# Table of Content

# THE LURE OF YVONNE

## REALITIES AND FANTASIES

It was a really a cheery bright night and the entire garden was awash with the bright, captivating light of the moon. Everything was so magical and surreal that the young man walking in the garden thought the whole thing was a mere fantasy. But he had had to pinch himself several times to be able to discern if the whole invitation from his lover was real at all. Though he was still very excited anyway as he had never even thought of something alluring and magical as a lovers' date outing in a beautiful garden of different exotic flowers under the moonlight before. The light cool breeze blew around him a bit colder, and he adjusted his night coat more tightly around his body. But his body was already feeling the heat of his excitement as he continued towards the meeting point where his lover told him to meet her. He wondered just what she had in mind as he walked more quickly and deeper into the gardens. For a reason, he couldn't remember where he had met her but he still knew that they had always known each other like since forever. He knew in his heart that he loved and cherished her with every fibre of his being and would always do everything in his power to please her, and which was why he completely trusted her on this late night meeting of theirs. He was greatly anticipating how pleasant the surprise she had promised him was really going to be and that has started to make his body tingle all over, making his groin tight. He shivered both with the whistling, cold breeze and his anticipation of meeting his love and started to softly mumble a love song to himself. He eventually got to their agreed meeting place; a very peaceful looking glade with a nearby bubbling stream. The glade was resplendent with more colourful flowers and their fragrance truly permeated the whole clearing with their different perfume. The whole scene was just exactly like a picture cut out of one of those fairy tales or fantasy movies. He breathed in the fragrance circulated by the clean, fresh air of the glade and sat down on a rock in front of a giant oak tree and waited for his girl. He leaned back against the tree and looked around, hoping to catch a glimpse of her but still he couldn't see anybody. He shrugged and waited till he started dosing off to the quiet, lulling sounds and cool breeze. It was not up to five minutes later when he was suddenly startled from sleep by a splash somewhere around the stream not that far to where he was sitting. His heart thumping wildly, he looked around and scanned the area he suspected the sound probably came from.

"Hey Yvonne is that you?" I'm right here" He called out but didn't get a response.

There was quiet for some time and he began to unwind, thinking it was likely a fish. Then this time there was the sound of a huge splash which really got him frightened.

'Shit! That wasn't just as mall fish. Or could it be something else?'He thought in alarm. He concentrated harder on the spot where the ripple of the last movement and sound occurred. It was not very long before a big tail swirled at a different but still not too far spot to where he was sitting. He stood up in trepidation and gulped when he started doubting what he was seeing swimming around in the stream. 'No it couldn't be'. He thought in shock. Or have mermaids started living in streams too?'

His fears were further confirmed when the body's outline became more revealed in the silvery cast of the moonlight. The watching boy could now really confirm that the strange figure he was seeing was indeed a mermaid. Scared but still curiously baffled and fascinated, he stood rooted to the spot he was as the magical creature, obviously sighting him, started to swim gradually with quiet, clean strokes to the stream bank towards him. On getting to where he was, her head (at least her body structure looked feminine to him as far as he could see) briefly poked out. She immediately disappeared into the water for a long while, making him start to wonder if he had not been actually hallucinating. And at that point he remembered the scary stories and myths he had read about of the full moon having psychedelic and psychotic effects if one stays under it for too long at night. He was proved wrong not long afterwards when her head once again poked out of the water before gradually rising to now fully reveal her alluring magical figure. In fact it was exactly like he first thought, just like a fairy tale, and what with the full illumination of the bright moonlight. He gulped as a part of his mind kept telling him to run because the whole thing just doesn't make sense while another part of him that was being overruled by his male hormones at seeing the rare, sexy and magical sight before him held him captive on the spot. The mermaid rose up till all her curvy, feminine figure stood before him in all sexy, wet glory. To him, the moonlight seemed to even shine magically brighter than before as her water pebbled skin shone like a stunning statue coming alive. The beautiful tail that playfully flashed and splitter the water behind her glittered like the deepest colour of jade. Though it was difficult to truly discern her skin colour from the distance where she was staying yet, but he could tell it must be absolutely smooth. Her wavy black hair cascaded down her body, alluringly covering her breasts and shoulders. Anybody seeing what he was lucky to be seeing right then would have readily thought a priceless portrait had just been given life, what with the magically entrancing way the moon seemed to be shining behind her naked figure in a stream within a beautiful glade of sweet smelling flowers.

There was absolute silence as both boy and mermaid stared at each other. He had even momentarily forgotten about his lover and the reason why he had come at that moment, his only focus on the fascinating seductress of the waters now standing in the stream before him looking at him. She flicked her tail again and started swaying and dancing. Her movements were more or less seductive as her silhouette gyrated wetly under the silvery cast of the moonlight over her. Nothing ever, not even if Jesus himself suddenly came down to him at that moment, can draw away his enchanted attention from the totally tempting sight before him. The mermaid danced for a few more minutes, all this while creating silvery ripples across the surface of the stream. Then abruptly she stopped, ran her fingers over her breasts before putting her right forefinger into her mouth and licked it in a 'I'm hot and horny gesture'. She faced him and pointed the finger at him, using it to beckon him to draw closer to her. Normally, his first reaction was that of fright and uncertainty like he immediately felt towards such gesture, but he still helplessly moved like an automaton towards her all the same. 'Damn what is it with we men and always falling helplessly like a mindless fool whenever a very beautiful and enchanting female is involved. Our brains would just stop working at all' He thought ruefully.

Frightened but excited at the same time, he walked towards her like he was being drawn. He reached the figure at the shallow part of the stream and started spluttering a speech as he could not help himself from being overwhelmed standing in front of a magical creature like her.

"Hmmm....heeeeem....hi...  hithere....m....miss...humm I'm looking for my girlfriend and I'm not sure if you might have seen her" He stopped and looked down in embarrassment.

The mermaid didn't say anything at first and then she suddenly burst into fits of uncontrollable laughter. The man was at first shocked at the sound before he shifted in confusion and tentatively bent to watch her face closely.

"Shit Yvonne! Is that you? Damn how... what...wh... fuck that was really a performance girl. I almost died of a heart attack you know" He said and waved his arms in bewilderment.

The mermaid, now obviously no other person nor a magical creature but his lover Yvonne, continued to laugh hysterically as she leaned on him for support.

"Heart attack you say? Or you meant to confess that you were so hot and hard for a beautiful stranger in tail that you totally forgot about your girlfriend and didn't even mind going down to the bottom of the sea, or this time a stream with a mermaid." She said between fits of mirth as she tried to breathe.

The boy was disgruntled but amused, "Well what can I say. You sure can give any real mermaid a run for her money with all the arrangements and performance. Damn girl I must say you really got me there." He laughed and pulled her towards him.

"Hmmm so it didn't even take you long to totally forget about me once you saw another female more enticing than I am, huh Sal?" She smiled but with a bit of disappointment inside her tone.

Sal held her so tight and close. Then he lovingly kissed her brow and said, "It won't happen again Yvonne. Even though you really wowed me with your mermaid performance but you remember I still mentioned that I was finding you. You will always be at the forefront of my heart and no mermaid, no matter how sexy or powerfully captivating, can ever erase you from it. I've always loved you and I shall always love you no matter how many beautiful mermaids it takes to drag me under the streams. Though I would much prefer you being the mermaid seducing me like this every night." He finished and chuckled as she giggled heartily.

Sal slowly raised her face and whispered, "From now on, you shall always be my little mermaid forever having me wrapped with the tail of her heart" And then he promptly plundered her lips with a hungry kiss.

She moaned and wriggled more closely against him as they duelled with each other's tongue. Their kiss was so intense that Yvonne did not even know when he quickly carried her to the bank. He continued kissing her before going down to her couple of rosy bosoms and equally ravaged them with his eager tongue and lips. She shook and moaned feverishly as she flicked her fake mermaid rubber tail in ecstasy. He continued feasting on her front globes as he gently dipped his hands underneath her costume to caress her wet pussy. Before long his ministrations had her gushing warmly against his strumming fingers drilling her hot tunnel. Yearning to taste more of her, he gave a feral snarl, gripped her rubber tail and rolled it off her skin. He also quickly made a short walk of his clothes before bending down to plunge his tongue into her sweet meadow. Yvonne cried out and gripped his head as he ravaged her hot, runny pussy smearing his mouth and chin with her musky juice. She soon shook from a strong orgasm as his fingers plunged in with his stabbing tongue. Not relenting, he took hold of his nodding cock and plunged it smoothly into her still hot and yearning kitty. As he fucked her under the moonlit glade, her voice mixed sweetly with the running stream in the background. The thought of his love under him in a beautiful garden as such, the special moment she had created and the absolute romantic feeling soon made his balls churning with hot cum. He groaned like a wounded bull as his own thick juice spurted hotly out of him.

But as he was about releasing, a really loud noise jabbed into his ears and Sal immediately woke up to his alarm clock back in his dormitory room as he had yet another one of his countless wet dreams about his best friend, Yvonne.

Sal angrily got up to clean up the mess he had created with his cum on his boxers and bed sheets before getting ready for the day's lectures. He sighed and shook his head in pity at himself. 'Oh no not again. For how long am I gonna do this?' He thought in exasperation. He got up to the bathroom to wash up when he caught his reflection in the mirror. Looking at himself, he thought he was not that bad. Standing a little bit below six foot, Sal looked like a fit athlete what with his routine participations in various sports and karate lessons. His stunning blue eyes were a killer according to many of the females he comes across. His light, dark hair was always ruffled in a cute way even as he always tried as much as possible to brush them down. He shrugged and fiercely decided that that day would be the last of his wet dreams and fantasies about Yvonne. He would just have to man up, walk up to her and finally declare his love no matter what it takes for him. Or is there anything worse that could happen to that? And then with that strong resolve, he got ready to hit the campus.

************************************************

*

Sal has always been deeply in love with his best friend Yvonne for as long as he could actually remember. Even though they had actually been very close since their freshman year and had been doing almost everything together, their relationship has always been nothing more than being platonic. He had saved her from a gang of muggers in an alleyway while coming alone from a party with his friends. She had gratefully accepted his hospitality for the night so she can get settled emotionally. It was not until the next morning that he discovered she also attended the same college like him, and also as a freshman. They had bonded from there and have since been inseparable. Though most still think they were romantically attached but they always laughed it off, stating that they were only very close friends. Though at one point, they might have felt some feelings for each other but none among them had truly dared to explore that area. It was really a baffling mystery to those around them. People usually decide whether Sal was not really into black girls or vice versa.

Sal saw and hears Yvonne calling him from afar as soon as he got around the humanities department. He could only stare hungrily at her deliciously ebony skin as she walked towards him cheerfully. She was almost his height but svelte and cute in a not too thin modellish sort of way. Her pert breasts were always firm as oranges in her clothes. But apart from her long, wavy black hair, it was her almond shaped brown eyes and long smooth legs that always made him lost. Her eyes were always as if they were lustily staring into his soul. Her legs too were always a killer for him. In short, she was the complete package to him but sadly she doesn't know how his feelings for her run deep. He had so gotten lost about thinking of her that he didn't hear what she was saying to him when he reached her.

"Hey! Hey! Earth to Sal. What world have you travelled to this time, huh?" She giggled as she slapped him lightly on the cheeks.

He sighed and forced himself to smile, quickly dispersing his lost look, "Oh what's up Yvonne. Hope you are good? Well I know you are coz you are always beautiful as always."

Yvonne rolled her eyes and giggled, "Yeah right. Flattery won't get you anywhere stud. So what are you up to today?"

Sal shrugged and replied, "Nothing much. Particularly don't have a place in mind. What about you, runny mouth?"

"Well I have a date today. But I would like you to meet him later. Do you think you can come around by then?" She asked.

Sal suddenly felt a burst of anger at that revelation. It was as if her news brutally punched him in the guts. He nearly doubled in pain at his lost chance of declaring to her how he truly felt.

"Hey you okay? You've suddenly grown pale all of a sudden" Yvonne asked with deep concern written all over her pretty, round face.

Sal quickly shook his head, "Nah I'm just having some stomach upset. Must be what I took for dinner. No worries Yvonne. We should catch up later. Need to go to the toilet right now."

Yvonne rubbed his shoulders, "Or should I come with you?" She asked.

"No you go ahead. We shall catch up this afternoon later okay."

Yvonne nodded, "Alright see ya later but call me as soon as you finish in the toilet alright? You know I'd be worried." She looked at him inquiringly once again and patted his back before leaving.

But only Sal knew his own inner pain as he watched her leave. He just knew that he had to avoid her for the meantime. He really felt like shit as he left for one of the outer and secluded toilet blocks around the campus premises. He got into one of them and stayed for a while. Still feeling disoriented, he opened one of the faucets there and splashed some water over his face till the horrible feeling went away. He breathed in and out for a while to calm and steady himself. After taking a piss and washing his hands, he left the restroom with a very sad feeling of dread and hopelessness. On getting outside, he suddenly got a whim of decision and changed his position towards the direction of home.

▪▪▪▪▪▪▪▪▪▪▪▪▪▪▪▪▪▪▪▪▪▪▪▪▪▪▪▪▪▪▪▪▪▪▪▪▪▪▪▪▪▪▪▪▪▪▪▪▪▪▪▪▪▪

And the remaining days of the week saw Sal trying to avoid Yvonne. And at those times he just could not avoid attending lectures, he would sullenly go to the campus so as to academically keep himself afloat. And as soon as he finished, he would quickly disappear to one of the secluded buildings around the campus premises to stay a while so he would surely not cross path with Yvonne. Though Yvonne had even tried blocking him by patiently waiting for him to be through with a particular lecture once she was done with hers, but Sal would quickly do as if he was in a rush, stating that he was having an important meeting with either his course lecturer or course counsellor, which he knew had started getting her astounded and progressively suspicious of his thoughts or intents. Though Yvonne had also tried calling his mobile several times but he deliberately made the calls to keep going to his voice mail. In fact, Yvonne had gone to his apartment to try and know what was actually going on with him but she still discovered she couldn't even locate or see him. Anytime she knocked or tried his door, it was always locked. Though it was not as if Sal was not always home whenever Yvonne came looking for him. Whenever it happens that he was actually home at times when she came, he would deliberately keep everything quiet behind closed doors as if he was not really there. In fact, he usually sneaked in at the times he knew she would either be on campus or must have probably left again after waiting futilely for him at his room's entrance without seeing him. And so the hide and seek game went on successfully for a while for Sal, and for the first time thanked the universe for making him not to be in the same department and faculty with Yvonne. But yet even at that, he still found it very difficult to dodge or throw her off completely. But despite his hurt, he did felt like a jerk for what he was doing and deep down he knew he was unnecessarily torturing the poor girl who was meant to actually be his best friend. After all he had been a totally lame guy and coward for not making his intentions known to her but that was what genuine feelings of love usually does to someone who has always been head over heels in feelings for someone precious and close like Yvonne.

Yvonne on the other hand was truly hurt from Sal's confusing actions and totally mad at him for not even trying to reach out or bothering to share whatever the hell was eating away at him. It had now been a week since his complaint of a runny stomach, and which was the last time they had talked to each other. She just could not fathom why Sal had suddenly resorted to such acts of cold shoulder because she had started getting convinced that that was what he had started doing because she had tried to reach out to him several times to no avail. Now they had reached the start of the second week of their seeming form of Cold War and Yvonne really thought that the madness just has to end between them. She realized how deeply she missed his company despite now having a boyfriend. She had intended to introduce her new boyfriend, Nate, to him and maybe the three of them could hang out together. At first she had momentarily thought maybe Sal was angry she had gotten a boyfriend but had casually laughed and waved it aside because she just could not imagine Sal being jealous just because of her getting a boyfriend or something for any reason. She just could not believe the thought that he was probably nursing any feelings for her. 'Or could he?' she thought in confusion and a momentary stab of yearning but laughed and shook her head. 'No, never it just could not be and neither can it work. I mean we are like brother and sister, right? She questioned no one in particular as her mind continued to roil in a tumult of different emotions.

She laughed out loud and shook her head to clear it, "Nope Sal is definitely not in love or jealous, and least of all definitely not with me. But I surely know that something is really eating away at him and whether he likes it or not today is the day I will find it out" She said and began to get ready for the day's lectures and campus activities.

Sal instantly noticed the absence of Yvonne around him that Monday and for the first time started wondering where she could be. A sharp jab of pain crossed his heart when the anger-inducing thought of her being with another guy formed in his head. He could imagine the hands caressing her sinfully smooth and beautiful, dark ebony skin which was exactly the colour of rich, dark chocolate. Those perfect, sexy legs and thighs always tantalizingly shown in her sexy short skirts being kissed upwards to her precious womanly core. Her delicious pert breasts with their wide areolae and thick, dark brown nipples being touched and su..... 'Damn it I should not be thinking of Yvonne that way. It ain't right at all' he shook in self rebuke and quickly cleared the annoying but tempting thought out of his head. But still that did not clear his mind of yearning for her. He figured that she would by now be very hurt and angry with him due to his uncalled for actions. He knew had not been honestly fair to her because she does not even know what is really bugging him or why he had been acting like a douche bag since the day she had revealed to him that she's got a date. He now realized how stupidly far his emotions had pushed him, and in so doing had hurt and pushed away his only best and precious friend; his lovely companion; his obsession; the enchanting haunt of his wet dreams all night long; the only girl to ever have absolute control over his feelings. He shook his head once again 'Oh no not again. I am no longer thinking straight'. Then Sal realized that the only way out of his torment is to try and mend things with Yvonne after the day's lectures. Heck he would readily suspend whatever other activities he has got scheduled for the day. He really needed to get home and make a call to Yvonne to forgive him and try to talk things through with her.

It was mid afternoon after lectures and there was a heavy downpour which had truncated the remaining of the day's activities and had led many rushing home and some still stranded in school. Sal had been one of the lucky ones to quickly leave the campus premises on time and had headed straight home as the sky was just about weeping down its own tears on them. He was disappointed and angry that he might actually not have the opportunity to speak to Yvonne that day. After thinking of what to do, he decided to make a call to Yvonne, hoping and praying she would at least pick up and give him a chance to say something. He had dropped his bag and books and was just about dialling her number on his phone when he was suddenly interrupted by a knock on his door. Wondering at what his neighbour would want in this heavy rain he grudgingly went to his door and looked through its peephole. The shock he got at unexpectedly seeing Yvonne at his doorstep at that point was much more than any he could have gotten supposing a loud thunder crash boomed over the building. He smiled ruefully, 'And here is the girl he was just about calling'. Many at times similar to that moment, it was always as if their minds work together at the same time. His brief hesitation prompted another knock from Yvonne and this time with a loud, exasperated voice.

"Please Sal I know you must be in there. Just open the door for me, please. I just want us to talk" She finished in an obviously distressed voice.

Sal's heart wrenched in pain at the thought of causing her more distress without her even knowing the reason. With a need as urgent as hers he quickly opened the door lock, removed the bolt and widely opened the door. It was as if a gust of happiness and relief had blown on him at that moment as he stared at her doe looking brown eyes and pretty face. She was wet and dripping all over from the rain and he instantly knew she had gone inside without a raincoat just because of him. It was at that moment that he knew one of the reasons why he loved her so much. Yvonne is a rare kind of girl that was bubbly with fun, good sense of humour, stunning in a way that was quietly alluring, and above all quite empathic to those she loves to a fault. He would have unashamedly confessed then that the days he had gone without her company had currently been the most hellish days of his entire life. He knew he just have to tell her how he felt, date or no date with a stranger.

Yvonne too on her part had been staring at him as she wrung out some of the water from her clothes. Though there really was nothing much to wring from her clothes because she mostly dressed in short Jean or silk skirts and low cut shirts, and never something too much or heavy. She doesn't know how to accurately describe her feelings throughout the time she was standing there before him. It was a boiling mixture of anger, happiness, relief, murder, hurt, empathy and even a hint of love in denial etc. Thus she did not know whether she should pounce on him with a big hug or descend on him with a slap to his douche brain. She made her decision once she finished with her hair. She neared him, looked at his face one more time and gave him a resounding slap on the face. But once she saw the red marks of her fingers on his face, she started regretting her rash action. It was just an extension of how he made her feel for his welfare and behaviour towards her in the past days. Yet she still went ahead to give him a whole lot of her pained mind.

"How dare you, Sal!" She shrieked in pure rage. "I mean what did I ever do to you to treat me as such? You don't pick your calls, you deliberately avoid me like plague and worst of all you never even bother to tell me what is going on. We are meant to be best friends, Sal and I don't think I truly deserve such treatments from you. Even if there's something I might have done wrong and I don't know about, you know you are always free to tell me. But stooping to this act Sal. And while we are at it, will you at least let me in? And you better start hoping to give me a very good and tangible reason why you have deliberately decided to treat me this way. Sal I was hurting and grieving, not knowing whether you are okay or not. I......I.........ermmm...... damn it Sal, but why?" She finished and started shaking with emotion as she breathed heavily after her outbursts.

Sal did not even bother to acknowledge the slap he had gotten. He knew quite alright that he totally deserved it and much more. He sighed clasped his hands together, "Yvonne I know you really have every right to be angry but I want you to know that I am truly sorry for all the pain and inconvenience I am sure I must have caused you since last week. I'm very sorry."

Yvonne shook her head, her curly and wavy shoulder length black hair swirling around her in sexy waves with tiny droplets of water falling from them. 'God she is so sexy that she does not even realize it half of the time, especially when her cute face twists in anger' Sal thought dreamily.

"Sorry you say? I mean is that all you have to say to me right now? As if you suddenly behaving like a total jerk was not enough. Now you think you can magically wish away everything you have done with a lame word like ordinary sorry? Oh hell no Sal Trent, I won't let you have your way, you jerk!" She finished and started punching him in the chests.

Even though her girly punches were just like massaging blows to his broad, muscled chests but he still felt the pain conveyed through them all over his body and particularly his heart. He watched her start to falter as her emotions finally took over her body. He quickly caught her hands as she could not hide her tears any longer.

"Let me go, you jerk. Please just let me go" She sobbed and finally collapsed on his shoulder as her body shook with her tears.

Sal held her close and gently patted her on the back as she wept out all the frustration he had caused her over the course of the week, all because of the stupid emotions he had let take over him and still refused to say out.

"I'm so sorry Yvonne. I now solemnly promise, from this moment on, never to hurt you in any way again. I will try and tell you anything I do feel even if it kills me. Please I just hope you would find it in your heart to truly forgive me and accept my apologies" He said softly.

Then a neighbour poked out his head, "Hey! Will you lovebirds try and keep it down? Someone is trying to have a decent sleep here, please."

Sal looked up and waved in apology, "We are truly sorry for disturbing your sleep mister. We are about done here."

"Better" The man grumbled and his head disappeared back into his apartment.

Sal's place was a new five-storey block of apartments that were built in brilliant architectural layers over each other in such a way that there was still privacy despite its connecting corridors and passages. It was a comfy and not too pricey comfortable place for a financially okay but prudent college student like him. Though his parents were rich but he was brought up to be disciplined and not to unnecessarily waste money. And naturally he was the kind of kid that detested vain lifestyle too. Though he had tastes and always made sure to use good and quality stuffs, but he still loved to be accountable for his spending, hence why his apartment was just the right and perfect place for his balanced lifestyle. It was not too cheap and drab for his standards and neither too unnecessarily gaudy and expensive for his cautious lifestyle. Though as the only kid, his parents had always made sure he does not lack for anything but they still beamed with pride at the disciplined, focused and compassionate young man he had grown to become. Yvonne too came from a comfortable home, though her parents were not as rich as that of Sal's but they were still financially comfortable. Yvonne has an elder sister who had already finished college and working out of states for one of the federal agencies as an auditor, while the last born in their family, their kid brother Rob, was at his third year in elementary school. She currently preferred to stay at one of the female dormitories on campus so she could be still be near her departmental colleagues, one of whom she shared room with, and also have access to girl gossips, girly times and flirting. Fortunately enough, Sal's apartment was not that far to the campus so it was always an easy walk for both of them whenever they see each other. And right now as they both shared their pains and emotions through their connected bodies, they knew their friendship runs deeper than the ordinary. It was as if they are now like brother and sister. But yet they could feel at the inner fringes of their heart that there was still that yearning to be more but neither want to take that bold, defining step for the fear that the precious bond they are currently enjoying from their friendship would be ruined. So each pretended to not feel anything and yet still hurt from their undeclared feelings, most especially Sal.

After Yvonne's sobs had subsided, they held each other for a while at the entrance before he took both of them into his room. He made her to sit down on one of his small sofas and went to make both of them mugs of hot chocolate. Both now sitting down with steamy mugs of cocoa, Yvonne had wasted no time in demanding for his explanations.

Sal took a deep breath and preceded, "Once again I apologize for everything Yvonne. It wasn't my intention to behave like an asshole. Also I........"

"Yeah you did behave truly like an asshole" Yvonne interjected.

"Yup, certainly" Sal agreed.

"And like a jerk"

"Truly ma'am"

"And a total douche bag"

"No lies right there"

"And a........"

Sal quickly interrupted her, "You see Yvonne, I know you have every right to be angry and vent it on me with any words you like but I still want you to know that I'm truly sorry and begging you to find it in that sweet heart of yours which is as lovely as your pretty face to forgive me. I'm truly and sincerely remorseful about all the upset and hurt I might have caused you. We have always told each other everything and it wasn't fair to just shut you away like that without reason."

Yvonne smiled and relaxed for the first time, "Awwhow sweet of you, my prodigal Sal. But flattery is not going to make me forget why you shut me out. So now explain." She said with a cute frown on her face.

God how could someone be so pretty, cute and caring at the same time? Sal swooned in thought. But as he was about uttering how he really felt to her his brain suddenly locked up. His mind got blank and no word could come out of his mouth. Had it been the situation was not tense, the comical look on his face would have been priceless and a source of good laugh for Yvonne but right now all she wanted to hear was the reason for his irrational behaviour. And she was starting to get confused and impatient at his hesitation.

She took a swallow of her chocolate and shrugged her shoulders at him, "Well I'm listening Sal"

Sal was already fuming at himself for the sudden speech block he was experiencing. He breathed in and tried to calm himself, smiled and proceeded to say something.

"My dad is seriously ill." He blurted.

Oh god, oh damn it now I have screwed up everything. Why did that have to come out of his mouth among all the other lies he should have said instead? But the damage has already been done and what was only left for him to do now was to try and finish what he had now started.

"Oh my god Sal! Why can't you tell me? You should have called or something. I mean yes we are yet to know our families but that doesn't mean we can't tell each other anything about them should the need arises in instances like this. If we can't do that then what are we friends for? But that aside, is he getting better?" She asked with genuine concern and worry written all over her face.

Sal sighed and thought 'Yes I've indeed blown everything up now with my stupid lie'. The anguished look on his face, though genuine, was absolutely mistaken for grief by Yvonne and her heart melted towards him.

"Sal I'm so sorry for being a bitch. Had it been you've told me about what has really been going on, there wouldn't have been any need for all this. I was just worried sick about the thought of anything bad happening to my best friend." She said and stood up to sit by his side on the sofa he was occupying.

His heart wrenching to pieces on her true concern and care about a lie only him knew he had told, he quickly shook his head to save her from further emotional anguish on a terrible lie, "No it's okay Yvonne. I truly appreciate your care. I just want you to know that your reactions towards my actions do not make you a bitch in anyway because you were only watching out for your best friend. And I always want you to know that you are still my best friend, now and always. I knew you would definitely be worried sick of this, so that is why I couldn't bear to tell you anything but all the same there was no excuse for what I did. So once again I'm deeply sorry. And I don't want you worrying again because my dad is now getting better, so no more clucking like a mother hen over me. This tough guy will never break, well that is if you are not around me anymore" He finished and they laughed warmly. At least he knew that most of what he said was true in a way after all.

Yvonne sighed happily and hugged him tight, "Yes you're right boy. I will always be your mother hen. I mean if I can't look after you, then who will?"

Then both of them laughed out loud. It had been such a while they had laughed happily together and the sound of their voices laughing in unison in the room was a sweet music to their ears. They separated and searched each other's eyes coincidentally. What even made the action more intensely felt was their dangerous proximity to each other on the sofa. Funny enough, it was not even awkward for them at all because all they could feel was an unexplainable but powerful energy around them that seemed hell-bent on drawing them closer. Despite the coolness of the weather, Sal gulped and sweated as the heat of passion between them began to rise to unbearable levels. He unknowingly licked his lips as he ravenously gazed at her pretty, succulent and lightly pink lips. Yvonne on the other hand just could not fathom what had suddenly gone wrong between them. All she knew at that crazy moment was that she and Sal were being dangerously drawn and tempted to break their barrier of friendship by closing the distance between them right there and then and seal it with a hungry kiss. But despite the obvious, strong sexual attraction they were feeling, both were still adamantly restraining themselves from taking the step that could redefine their relationship, or probably destroy it. It was a sort of emotional stalemate as both boy and girl continued to breathe in light gasps as they eyed each other with looks of hunger and sexual torture. Just as both were likely to succumb to their real feelings, the ringtone of Taylor Swift's Haunted rang out in the thick, heated silence of the room. Startled and disoriented, both of them quickly distanced themselves and stood up. They looked around and discovered the phone ringing was Yvonne's. She quickly went for it and checked her screen. She immediately gave an alarmed hiss and turned to Sal.

"Damn it! I was meant to go deliver a package from my mom to an uncle of mine at the county hospital around this time. It was my mom calling to probably know if I have delivered it to him. And it is really urgent he receive it today. I have totally forgotten about it. Please I'm so sorry I have to go now Sal. Hope you will be alright?" She asked as she finished the remaining of her cocoa and picked up her bag pack and made to leave.

Sal shook his head and replied, "Oh no, it's alright. But it is still raining heavily though so why don't you just take my raincoat and umbrella with you. I'll collect both back tomorrow on campus, okay?"

"Oh I'm so grateful Sal but I think I'll prefer only the umbrella. I'm already wet from the rain anyway so there won't be any need for the raincoat, but thanks all the same Sal. You really are a lifesaver." She said and smiled at him.

Sal beamed but waved her words aside, "Oh come on now Yvonne. You and I both know the reason for almost forgetting to deliver that package was me. So the least I can do is get you something to prevent you from getting drenched in the rain."

She frowned but lightly punched him on the shoulder, "Hey who says I shouldn't be here? You know I never joke with my friends' welfare, let alone you of all of them. We're partners in crime and merit, remember? And I fully expect you to do same for me when it's your turn, comprende?" She finished with a terrible French intonation that made both of them burst into fits of laughter again.

Sal then escorted her downstairs to the exit. It was still heavily raining when they got outside and she instantly unfurled the umbrella. She turned around and they smiled at each, "So see you tomorrow then, partner" She said.

"Yeah see you tomorrow and my sincere gratitude for dropping by. It really means a lot to me Yvonne."

"Nah don't mention. Bye and see you" Then she turned to leave.

Then Sal called out "I'll give you a call and make sure to be careful from slipping"

"Okay" She loudly answered back.

Then he did the unthinkable that got both of them surprised, especially himself.

"I love YOU" he partially shouted.

Oops! What the hell was that? He thought in shock.

Yvonne too had heard him, but she was not really sure if she had heard him right due to the noise of the falling rain.

She looked back and stared at him intensely, her heart thumping with fear and something like hope and expectation, "Is there anything else you want to say to me, Sal?" .She shouted back. "Thought I heard you say something."

Sal vigorously shook his head and shouted, "Nope I didn't. Just saying you should be careful"

Yvonne nodded, "Okay alright then. I will. See you later tomorrow" She said and carefully made her way towards where she could board a taxi.

Sal stamped his foot in frustration and anger. 'Damn you fool, Sal. In fact you are the stupidest of all love drunk fools. Imagine blowing up your chance of declaring your heart to her again. Fat chance in hell will you ever get the opportunities you have gotten today'

He sighed tiredly in resignation and left for inside the exit. Meanwhile, Yvonne was feeling relieved but disappointed at the same time. She believed that what Sal claimed to be what he said was definitely different from what she thought She had heard from him. She looked back again and could not find him at the entrance. She shrugged 'Well maybe he was right after all and I must have been hearing things that were not real'

Things had now become settled once again between Sal and Yvonne and they were back to their normal inseparable selves. Though neither believed there should be anything more from the other person. Yvonne, despite the special bond and tingling feelings she does get whenever she was with Sal or when they touch, still forced herself to believe that Sal was not really into black girls. Heck, she had not even seen him with any girlfriend so to speak, and the ones she had usually found around him were white girls. This made her close friendship with him to still be an enigma to many others around them and including her. Though it was not as if he was racially choosy or anything but that has mostly been what was happening. But despite that, he does get his fair share of girls of every race drooling over him. And yes Sal, despite his cool and reserved demeanour, could easily pass as a suitable candidate for a Mister Campus pageant. The same could be said of Yvonne. The only thing that made her different was her extroverted, naughty and playful ways. Though she was as disciplined as Sal, if not more, but she just loved to be jovial and fun to be around. But another storm of contention has started looming and which might bring an irreparable damage to the bonded friendship they both shared.

They were now at their sophomore year and academics have started getting a bit more serious and tedious. Sal was studying programming and software engineering while Yvonne was studying digital marketing and advertisement. Though they still find the time to hang and fool around a bit but it seemed that more works coupled with extracurricular activities have lessened the time they usually have as freshmen in the previous year. Yvonne had informed Sal that it was high time he met her first boyfriend on the campus. Though she claimed there had been the start of mutual interests towards the end of their first year, but it seems they have only recently started to kindle their flame of romance. She had also said that the guy in question was also a departmental colleague. Sal, not wanting another situation of where one person would be the reason another person was in distress, decided to take everything in stride and be determined to be happy for her, even if the happiness does not reach his heart. Besides he thought they were adults and not getting younger so one must endure and take life as it comes. Not everything always works according to one's plans anyway. And so he had put on a show worthy of the Oscars the day Yvonne came with the lucky guy for a form of introduction. Sal had smiled at the appropriate time and talked when he needed to. Even though Yvonne could not find any fault in the way he comported himself. In fact she was kinda impressed by his cool attitude but at the same time felt hurt that he would just be cool with everything. She absolutely knew the way she was thinking was not right, hence unfair to Sal but she just could not change the feeling that he should at least have showed some jealousy, bitterness, a frown or something that he truly felt something for her. Sal on the other hand was preoccupied with talking with the boyfriend, whose name was Fred, and trying to detect some hidden faults or errors. Though Fred seemed okay on the surface but yet he could not help but feel something was off about him, kind of like being fake and subtly vain or something. But he shrugged it off as a case of emerging envy and he definitely don't want to be the guy that would be labelled as an envious asshole spoiling his female friend's relationship. Though he had first hesitated to tell Yvonne how he felt simply because he had a hunch, but he knew there was no way he could just leave her to a wolf's trap. So he called her and they chatted and joked before he briefly told her that she should be careful of Fred and that he did not trust him.

"Hmmm and what really gives you that hunch, Sal. Or do I detect jealousy talking?"

Yvonne heard his audibly tired sigh from the other end and deeply regretted her statement.

"Look I only just wants you to be okay and be careful. I think that is what really matters to me, nothing else." He said.

Yvonne felt a burst of gratitude and a strange kind of warmth at his words.

"I was only pulling your legs Sal. But I really appreciate your concern and I'll make sure to be very careful, right dad?" Her light banter quickly lit up the mood between them and they laughed warmly from both ends.

"So I guess I'll be seeing you guys around soon. Please do take care of yourself. Bye for now." Sal said and cut the call.

Once Sal disconnected, she suddenly felt the brief warmth and joy she had been enjoying some minutes ago evaporate. And she instantly knew the cause. She longingly looked at Sal's number on the screen of her phone. Now She knew she cannot just deny the fact that talking with Sal has always been fun and exciting. Apart from the fact that she enjoyed always making him the butt of her jokes, she wickedly loved the way she strutted around him whenever they were together, stylishly teasing him with her signature short skirts and low cut shirts as he watched her with a form of passionate hunger that excited her. No man yet, not even Fred really looked at her that way, and for the first time she started to actually think whether using Fred as a form of escape from her feelings was indeed the correct choice. But as much as she loved the way Sal adores her with his looks and close friendship, she was very frightened that what they shared might not be as great if they suddenly decided to turn their relationship to a romantic one. There are times she even mused whether their friendship could be what is labelled as platonic but they have not been intimate with each other at all ever since both of them have met one another. Even though they had really been free among themselves but never have they crossed that sacred boundary of friendship into a romantic or erotic one?

Though deep down, she felt Sal was probably feeling the same way too and even more like she always suspected, but she does not think it would augur well for them if they decide to test those waters. In truth, she really cherished their close friendship and she would love it to be that way between both of them. And yet she kept feeling a deep yearning; a void of emotions whenever Sal was absent from her. Indeed the first semester of their sophomore year have really been hectic and occupying, but she always make sure they see or talk on phone almost every day. Sal, despite his bottled feelings, has also been keeping up their communication as frequently as possible. She only hoped he would understand as she does that they should only see each other like family and nothing else. It was only by that she believed they would forever maintain their true closeness.

Or is it?

Sal saw a not too shocking scene one day as he drove to town one evening in his truck. He had seen Fred groping some strange women on the streets and noisily taking booze and what was obviously weed and drugs with some rough looking dudes and rednecks. It was really a crowd of bad company that he would not want a part of. Normally he detested violence and unnecessary confrontation and besides they were all adults anyway. But his major concern was for his best friend Yvonne. He always tried to respect other people's decisions and privacy but what he was seeing was unavoidably making his blood boil. He shook his head as he drove around towards their side. So this is what Yvonne now deserves, huh? He parked a little bit away from them and approached.

"Hey Fred what's up man. How you doing?" He said in greeting.

Fred, now hugging two garishly tattooed ladies to him, looked up but barely acknowledged him. "Hu... hu yes what the fuck do you want? Or this place looking like a fancy campus to yer?" It was obvious that he was already stoned as his formerly undetected Southern drawl became evident in his slurred speech.

Some of the rowdy gang loitering around were already closing in on them. Sal was not in the least bit worried because he knew he could take almost all of them in a fight either with weapons or fisticuffs. Apart from already achieving a black belt in his Karate lesson, he was currently in training in special martial arts of disarming, defence and combat. But he was not there for a fight with them. That was not his concern and would never be good for reputation anyway.

"I knew you were fake the first time I saw you. But looking at you now, I just can't fathom what Yvonne actually sees to date the likes of you at all. But it's not her fault any way because you are really good at pretending coz you are a fake and will always be one. I mean just look at you cavorting around and doing drugs and shit when you have a fine, caring lady at home? Christ you motherfucker better not try to be near her again or else........"

"Or what, huh? You pussy whipped asshole? You sure gat nerve bumping 'round in here like a hamster and talking shit o'er my face. Well that sweet black ass is all mine and ain't nothing you gon do about it, sissy." He laughed to his face and smacked the asses of the two women with him.

"Hey boys, ain't it time to have some juicy, black pussy to oil my Johnny boy righ' here?" He continued to laugh as he crudely made lewd and sexually suggestive movements with his dick.

And the hooligans around him hooted and wolf whistled gleefully as they laughed.

Sal was at once livid with rage at the deliberate use of foul language Fred had used to address Yvonne's race. He gritted his teeth and approached the annoying guy with his fists clenched into strong, muscular balls.

"What..the....hell....did....you......just......call....her?" Sal slowly stressed his question in a voice showing great anger that he barely acknowledged the redneck touts now drawing out their weapons, ready for a fight.

Even though the scenario was like seven to one but the most sensible among them were obviously being cautious in approaching him due to the power and professional fighting stance they could see yearning to be put to use through his body.

Even Fred looked rattled at the oozing confidence of Sal as he approached him and he was thankful in his mind that his cronies were around him. But in order to appear fearless, he spit on the floor near Sal, grinned and replied, "Yeah you heard me, superman" By thenhe had pushed the two women from him, and had taken a crooked, pathetic stance of combat with the fear in his eyes becoming more visible.

Suddenly the whole anger disappeared from Sal and he burst into uncontrollable laughter. Fred and his gang were caught unawares and nothing short of surprised at his abrupt change of purpose. Then when they realized it seemed they were being mocked, they started to get angry once again and bared their weapons.

"Hey asshole, what the fuck is so funny, huh?" Fred asked in anger.

But Sal was already done with them as he continued to laugh towards his truck. He could see he no longer had the need to engage them. They are only a bunch of pathetic losers trying to form tough. He gave them the finger as he drove off and they swore at him in return. He knew he just had to tell Yvonne as soon as possible that her so-called boyfriend was a worthless jackass who does not deserve her attention, let alone love from her.

<hr>

Even though Sal has got many things to do on that day, he just could not wait to speak to Yvonne so as to warn her on the treacherous path of relationship she was towing before it became too late. He called her mobile phone and it rang for a while before it dropped. He called again and again until it was picked at the fifth ring.

"Hello there Sal or should I call you Sally? Gosh what a real sissy name for a man. So to what do we owe this so important call?"

Sal controlled the sudden rush of anger in him as he heard the stupid voice of Fred on the line, "Hey how are you doing my scared little hillbilly. So you are the one picking the calls now, eh? Or you are really scared of what's gonna happen if I spill the beans on you? I can still come and beat your fake, cowardly asses over you know. Let Yvonne know you are nothing but a merely lucky white thrash who is nowhere near as valuable as the next dog crap on the streets" Sal answered and laughed derisively.

Fred was already fuming from the other end when Sal heard some interruption and exchange of words before the phone was taken by Yvonne from the other end.

"Hello there Sal. It has really been a while. And what's up with you and Fred again?"

"Look Yvonne, I am calling to tell you about something very important and urgent. That is all. And besides I have been calling you for a while now and you did not pick until that your asshole of a boyfriend did."

"Hey Sal you know I won't allow you to talk like that about Fred to me. Please if not for him at least respect him on my behalf. And I was not with my phone when I went to ease myself. It was with Fred."

"Well he was asking for it anyway. So how can we talk? It is really important."

"Well I think I am hearing you quite clearly now."

"Look Yvonne, if it is not that important then I would already be telling you now on phone, but it is what only you and I can discuss one on one facing each other."

Yvonne sighed on her end, "Alright then let me give you directions to where Fred and I are currently."

"What? You want me to come there to meet you while that.....that......look can't you and I even talk alone again Yvonne?" Sal asked with exasperation.

"You know I have a boyfriend now. Things are now changed. And besides would it not look odd if I should just leave with you, even though you are my best friend, and leave my boyfriend behind? It does not speak well you know"

"Alright fine. If that is the way you want it. It is just talk anyway and once it is done, I would be on my way."

Yvonne gave him the location and ways to take and they finished the call. Yvonne felt guilty and terrible at talking to Sal like he was a stranger but she still could not believe that he hated Fred so much so as to come and lie against him right before her. Even though she did not know what to believe and still confused about everything, she does not want anything to come and ruin what she was now enjoying with Fred and so far so good she was yet to see him behave uncouthly towards her in any way. She only hoped Sal would exercise restraint when he eventually comes. Sal located them ten minutes later at a private park a little bit far to campus.

Indeed a perfect, private place for lovers in love, Sal thought wryly. He parked a little bit beside Yvonne's Chevy and alighted. There were some other couples and lovers scattered here and there around the park. He spotted Fred and Yvonne under a birch tree and promptly approached them. His heart twisted in undeniable jealousy as he saw them holding hands and laughing. He steeled his mind, took a deep breath and quickly walked down to them. The earlier he gets the talking done the better. They both looked up as he neared their position.

"Hey there Yvonne. So can I see you now, in private of course, if you do not mind?" He said and totally ignored Fred.

Yvonne sighed and shook her head at the two of them and looked at Fred. Then she looked back at Sal.

"Please Sal, can't we at least talk about this between ourselves?"

Sal did not move from his spot, "Well it is a talk only between you and I but if you do not want to hear it, then fine. It isn't that I do not have other tangible things to do with my time. So what is it going to be Yvonne?" He finished and stared into her face, still totally ignoring Fred.

Yvonne sighed and briefly talked quietly with Fred who nodded at her before she left to meet Sal. Sal led her a bit to be the front that was not out of eyesight but a bit of earshot of Fred and other people.

Yvonne folded her arms and looked at him inquiringly, "So what is so important that could not be talked on phone and in front of my boyfriend, huh Sal?"

Sal quickly made a calming gesture with his hands, "Hey calm down Yvonne. I mean it's still me right here in front of you and you keep on treating me like a total stranger. Have we really become that distant that we can no longer share a secret or talk to one another in private like we used to before?"

Yvonne unfolded her arms and softened at his words. She did felt she had not been treating her best friend fairly nowadays, especially since when he had asked for a private talk between them. It was just that she had started building something beautiful with Fred that she just doesn't want anything to ruin that sweet reality for her. Though she was fully aware of Sal's full intent of always watching out for her like they do for each other, especially in the past, but she was already getting tired of the never-ending enmity between him and Fred. She only wanted peace and harmony between them for a change.

"Look I'm sorry Sal. It's just that Fred and I are trying to build something beautiful from our relationship and I really do not want anything to jeopardize that or anything else I hold dear, including you Sal. You are still my best friend and I really want you to be happy for me like the way I would be if you find someone special in your life too." She said and touched his shoulder.

"Well you do know I will always be happy for you Yvonne. And nothing can change that no matter what. Still, it is not possible for me to seeyou walking into a lie decorated as a false package of happiness and keep quiet about it. I believe that is what best friends should rightly do for each other, no matter how ridiculous as it may sound or look. And I am telling you at this moment with the utmost sincerity of my heart and proof that that guy right there is bad news. Yeah it may sound crazy or unbelievable to your love-sick ears, but that is the absolute truth Yvonne. Though I have been having doubts about what I had initially suspected about him the day you introduced us to each other but I kept waving it away until this encounter I had with him in town two days ago. In fact had it been we have not drifted a bit apart from each other these days, it is possible I might have told you what Fred had done and said that particular evening." Sal finished and then proceeded to tell her what transpired between him and Fred on that night.

Yvonne listened to him at first with unconvinced amusement until he mentioned the insulting wordhe claimed Fred had used. Her face immediately clouded in anger and her body stiffened.

"What did you just say Sal?" She whispered as she shook with anger.

Sal, now happy that she was finally listening to him, repeated the word he said Fred had used to address her. Though he never had the intention of telling that part to Yvonne but he knew had no choice other than to use it to catch her full attention to how serious what he was saying was. He smiled gleefully at the bashing Fred would now get from her when she called him to come over. Now is the time to put an end to this charade of relationship, he thought.

But things never went according to plan as Fred was asked by Yvonne in a dangerous but quiet voice if all what she had heard from Sal was indeed true. But Fred was as cunny as he was fake and narrated that indeed Sal saw him among his friends that evening but that it was only a harmless gathering of frat students who were discussing among themselves that he saw, and it happened that a bunch of rough looking fellows were around the vicinity but far from them at the time. He added that Sal had seen him laughing and having a good time among his frat friends and had decided to pick on him, even intimidating and threatening them with his martial arts capabilities. He solemnly narrated how it was the rough looking bunch that had unbelievably rescued them from him.

"And as for the use of such an insulting word, I must really say wow man you must really be hell-bent on destroying the loving relationship Yvonne and I have to have stooped so low in concocting such despicable words in order to frame me. Look Yvonne, I know you guys go way back as best friends, but I am really terrified that this is the kind of guy you have been calling a true friend. I mean can you just listen to all the illogical and terrible things he has been saying just so to turn your mind against me and tear us apart?" Fred practically raised his voice uttering the last words in alarm. Some of the people have by then started staring at them.

Yvonne, now openly weeping, turned to the now totally stunned Sal as his face turned white from the sudden turn of events. He still could not believe Fred had just outsmarted him. He had cleverly removed the cloth of integrity right from under him and had made him fall right down on his ass. What even made everything more painful was the fact that Yvonne, who used to cherish him as a close friend, was now staring at him with hurt, hatred and disappointment. He was suddenly so helpless he could not talk. But out of the desperation to just say something in the hopes of salvaging the situation, he opened his mouth out of sheer willpower just to utter something.

"Yvonne, please I swear with everything I have and our true friendships that all what he said are nothing but lies. Please just believe me." Sal managed to say with all the look of anguish and pain in the world clearly written all over his handsome face.

Though she didn't say anything at first, but somewhere inside, despite the cloudy veil of anger and hurt currently covering her face and thinking, Yvonne still noticed the sad look on Sal's face as he tried to prove his innocence, and funny as it may sound due to her feelings at that moment, it really wrenched her heart knowing fully well she was totally liable for everything. No matter how much it hurt though, she knew the best thing concerning this Fred business for now was for both of them to give themselves some space for a while. And despite the pain she was feeling at Sal's betrayal, she still valued her friendship with him far too much to risk it on an impulse or a word whether she still does not know whether it was truly used by whom or what.

"Please just leave Sal." She said softly.

Sal hesitated and stretched his hands towards her, still hoping for something, anything from her.

"I SAID LEAVE!!! JUST GO!! I DON'T WANT TO SEE YOUR FACE AGAIN!!" She screamed, attracting the more stares from those nearby.

"Please just go Sal, Please." She finished softly and then finally succumbed to her emotions as she sobbed openly on Fred's shoulders.

Fred briefly looked at him with a satisfied smirk and instantly changed his expression to an angry one, "You heard her man. She said you should leave now" He said a bit too loudly as he continued to rub Yvonne's back in consolation.

Sal, even though relishing breaking all his jaw if given the chance, was already aware that he was attracting unnecessary attention and stares, looked longingly at the crying Yvonne and turned to leave. Nobody saw his own tears of pain and sadness as he entered his vehicle.

Over two and a half weeks had passed since that unfortunate day at the park, and the situation between Yvonne and Sal had not improved; in fact, it had gotten worse. Their usually easy-going friendship had become awkward, and though he couldn't be certain, Sal got the distinct impression that Yvonne was now avoiding him. Talk about a reversal of situation. He had tried to reach to her a week after the incident but she was neither not picking his calls nor answering his messages on all channels. Though Sal didn't want to scare her off, but he didn't want their friendship to just fizzle out and die simply because of a stupid misunderstanding. He really wanted to mend things with the girl that meant the whole world to him even if nobody else, including her knows. So on Friday of the third week, he resolved to take matters into his own hands. He knew that Friday afternoons were the one day of the week that Yvonne didn't have some activity to run off to immediately, so he figured this would be as good a time as any to corner her and work things out. If she wouldn't talk about it, he would. Today, after all academic activities might have ceased, he would broach the subject and try his possible best to make Yvonne let things smooth out between them.

Of course, with such an important mission at hand, the day crawled by at a painfully slow pace. Sal could barely focus on the droning voice of his software algorithm lecturer, preoccupied as he was with the far more important task of rehearsing exactly what he would say to Yvonne in his head. He envisioned the scene over again and again - they would talk, she would gladly accept him back, and then he would lean in and hug her sexy body, breathe in her lovely Jasmine fragrance that he so much loved, then they would look at each other soulfully and maybe share a tender kiss that would gradually grow more and more passionate as their mutual attraction exploded...the long-awaited ending of lectures jolted him back to reality. Daniel practically leapt out of his seat, making a beeline towards Yvonne's faculty, which thank goodness was not far from his own, and waited around her department to catch her lovely voice. Finally, he heard it: the sweet voice with its slightly musical lilt reached his ears, causing his stomach to do flip-flops. Sal paused and took a full breath, trying to properly steady himself. Hey now, you know you can do this. You just have to. She's beautiful and probably still mad at you right now, but you'll never know if she'll be yours until you ask her despite that douchebag Fred. Taking one last breath, he made his decision resolutely, and made his way down the hall of the department until he spotted her among some of her female friends. He greeted all of them and they responded warmly, too warmly because many of them had been crushing on him since their freshmen year. Sensing he had come for Yvonne, they quickly excused them and told Yvonne they would see her later tomorrow.

She didn't say anything, so he assumed she was waiting for him to talk. He requested that sheat least let them go somewhere a bit less noisy to talk. She nodded and followed him to a quieter area of the department.

"Hello Yvonne. I hope you are good?"

"Yeah trying to. Sowhat's up Sal? Why have you come here?" Her voice sounded slightly strained.

"Not much. I was wondering if we could talk, if you're not busy?"

"Sure, I've got twenty minutes before leaving. What's on your mind?"

Ok, she seemed warmer now, more receptive to hearing him out. That could only be a good thing, right? He took another deep breath, trying desperately to muster up all the confidence he possessed.

"Well, I just want you to know that all what happened that day was not meant to transpire like that. It was my fault and I am so sorry to have caused you much pain"

"Okay. So what else?" The happiness had gone from her voice, replaced by a brusque, almost harsh tone.

Sal felt his heart sink. Still, he had to persevere, so he forced himself to go on. "Well, I just wanted to say..."

He was cut off by the sound of footsteps approaching behind him, and Yvonne calling out cheerfully, "Fred!" He could hear the happiness in her voice, and it tore at him that Fred was now worthy enough to make her happy and he wasn't. It tore at Yvonne too; she felt like an absolute bitch, but she had to nip this fantasy she thought they used to have together in the bud. Ok, so if she was completely honest with herself, it was her fantasy too - the memory of how it had felt when they held hands, hugged each other whenever one of them needed comfort, how his touch had secretly made her flush with heat from head to toe, causing a delicious ache between her thighs each time she remembered it - but that didn't matter. You didn't trade on a solid friendship for a few mind-blowing orgasms or lofty fantasies.

Fred came to a stop in front of Yvonne and Sal.

"Hey honey," he said, flashing a pleasant grin.

Yvonne smiled back, her expression the perfect mix of coy and flirtatious, flipping her long, curly dark hair over her shoulder for added effect.

"What's up?" she asked.

"My frat is organizing a bash this weekend, starting from tonight at a specially booked guest house and I assure you that there is gonna be lots of fun. And besides, we have been working our asses off these past weeks so I think it is high time we unwind. So what do you say, my dark princess?"

"Sure!" she exclaimed, momentarily forgetting how awful she felt about Sal.

"You can come too man. You know no hard feelings and the likes" Mike added, directing the comment at Sal.

"What? Oh. Thanks," he said, half-heartedly. He had been lost in thought, berating himself for even daring to hope that he stood a chance with Yvonne at this point.

"Anyways, I've gotta go set up, but I'll see you tonight," said Fred, giving Yvonne a wink and a hot kiss, making her heart skip a beat as he walked off.

She giggled warmly as he swaggered off on the departmental corridor towards the exit .

"I still find it hard to believe Fred is a hooligan as you claimed Sal but I'm ready to let bygones be bygones. You really need to start getting happy for me you know" she asked, and turned to stare into his green eyes.

"Oh yeah, sure Yvonne. Truly happy," he replied dryly. If she had noticed his complete lack of enthusiasm she didn't try to show it.

She folded her arms as she continued to stare at him.

"So, you wanted to talk to me about something?" she asked, as casually as possible.

"Oh. It's not important, forget about it."

With that, he turned and walked away, wanting to get away from her before he completely broke down and made himself look even more pathetic. Yvonne watched him leave, her heart heavy in her chest. She wanted so badly to call out to him, to tell him to come back so that they could sit down and talk and go back to the way things were between them, even if it went against all the rationalizing she'd been doing to make herself feel better all week. If indeed she was doing the right thing, then why did it make her feel like scum? This line of thinking seemed dangerous, so she quickly squashed all feelings of guilt, focusing instead on her outing tonight with Fred. Packing up her bag quickly, she made the impulsive decision to skip late evening exercise practice. Even though it was highly out of character for her to even consider skipping an extra-curricular activity, she justified it by telling herself that she needed all the time she could spare to get ready. Tonight, she wanted to look hot enough to blow Fred's mind.

The night was really stormy and the thunder and lightning kept crashing all over. The sheets of rain continued drumming relentlessly without mercy. But despite the seemingly angry commotion of the late night weather, Yvonne drove desperately, battling the rainstorm and going as if a demon was after her. She fervently hoped and prayed that she meets Sal at home. Oh how could she have been so stupid to fail to see the signs, and most especially from her best friend who had been trying to warn her to be careful? The tears threatened to fall and blur her vision but she quickly had to shake them off so as not to disturb her driving. All her hopes and fantasies had come crashing down on her. She had indeed been sowing her seedon the wrong path. She reached Sal's apartment even as the rain continued to beat down in large sheets. She was so disoriented and agitated that all she could do was to only wrap herself up partially before running up into the entrance of the down floor's main door. Thankfully it was only closed but not locked and she quickly ascended the stairs in no time to Sal's apartment on the third floor. She fumbled in her bag for the keys, inwardly grateful for Sal forcefully getting the ones to his apartment for her a year ago. Oh what could she do without him? Sheat last found the right one, and let herself in. Once inside, she stripped off her raincoat and wet shoes and immediately shuffled over to his freezer and took out some Mama Bells' Chocolate Fudge ice cream cake. Ah the true cure for a lost and pathetic soul likes herself. Then she hastily grabbed a spoon nearby and hungrily shovelled a large scoop into her mouth. She pulled out a glass and headed over to the new portable bar in the living room, pouring herself the strongest liquor she could find. As the fluid burned down her throat she took the container with her back to one of the couches, where she sat on the floor and had a 'spur of the moment' meal at 1 am early in the morning. Once the alcohol had set in she found the tears rolling down her face as she came to terms with the end of the lie she had been building castles on; her short term relationship with that lying, worthless, pig Fred. And now she could only find refuge in the house of the only person, apart from her family, who had ever been caring, truthful, loyal and probably used to be in love with her that she had treated like thrash and chosen to humiliate just because of her stupid, irrational fear and idiotic willingness to believe in a lie all because she does not want to yield to the true feelings she had equally been nursing in her heart. And here she was, eating consolation food and drinking herself to stupor just to forget her grief in the same house of the person she now fully realized had probably been in love with her like since forever. Her body wracked with more sobs as she was overtaken with another gush of overwhelming sadness.

Sal suddenly woke up with a terrible fright from a very horrendous dream. In the dream, he had found himself playing with Yvonne on a right and stunningly beautiful Island and they had been happy and contented until the bright sky suddenly darkened over with a gloomy, ominous cloud that overshadowed everything. The island started to turn black and hot with magma and soot as its beautiful trees and plants started to wither and die. In their confusion, they were suddenly captured by demonic looking beings with huge breasts. He tried to fight them off but they were just too many and strong for him and so he was easily overpowered. They descended upon Yvonne and started carrying her away with them as she desperately called out his name while the remaining proceeded with defiling his body. He shouted and screamed for Yvonne but he kept on being submerged by huge breasts and demonic pussies as hot as napalm before he gave a panicked cry from his sleep. What kind of dream was that? He thought in confusion and looked down at his body to see he was covered all over in sweat. He stretched out and groaned as he worked out the stiff muscles his body. He shook his head to clear it and that was when he noticed the sound of a raging rainstorm falling outside his room for the first time. Looking at his bedside digital clock, he noticed it was just fifteen minutes past one in the night. He yawned tiredly and pushed himself to go shower off his sweat of fright. He thought he heard another sound beneath the ones being made by the heavy rain but shrugged it off as just the wind probably playing tricks with his ear.

Six minutes later, Sal shut off the shower and heard another sound, this time a sort of clatter clearly coming from the direction of his kitchen. Puzzled, he listened for several minutes more and when no other sound came out again he decided to ignore it, putting it down to exhaustion. He pulled on his pyjamas and a plain black T-shirt and sunk into his double bed. He reached for the remote for his big screen TV, one of his many presents to himself after successfully programming a series of hacking code algorithms for digital locks and keys for a company. The deal, despite paying now in thousands of dollars, would easily make him a millionaire in some years to come. In fact he had many more ideas and inventions in the works that if implemented successfully would surely turn him to a billionaire straight out of college in no time. Those are one of the good news he had intended to share with Yvonne before she suddenly decided to start putting a distance between them because of that good for nothing fucker named Fred. He sighed and quickly focused his attention on the TV before him. He was mindlessly flicking through channels when he once again heard more noises coming from his kitchen. Convinced this time that something odd was definitely going on in there, he jumped out of bed and quietly went to check it out with his combat cudgel. He let his eyes adjust a little bit first to the darkness before flipping on the light switch. He looked around and saw nothing at first before turning around the corner and stopped in his tracks. Had it been it was a sick, older person, he or she would surely have had a heart attack.

"What the....... Jeez! Yvonne is that you? You gave me a shocker. Wha...what are you doing there on the floor at this time of the night?"

For a second he stood watching her in silence. She looked like she'd been crying, and her usually immaculate black, wavy hair looked slightly dishevelled. She was sitting on his kitchen floor in a tight black dress along with the five inch heels, guzzling his vodka and ice cream cake. He observed the exquisite shaped, ebony-skinned creature and, just as he was about to say something, she looked up at him with her so adorable doe eyes.

"I have broken up with that bastard, Sal" she sighed, pouring herself another drink.

"Oh God. How?.....why?... I mean you guys were still together this evening. What really happened Yvonne? Oh and he better not have touched you" Sal growled menacingly andsat down on the floor with her.

Yvonne weakly nodded, "No he didn't though he would have loved to. But the way he and his friends talked about me like I was a piece of black pussy for the pleasure of taking. He did not even bother to defend or honour my person. The things he said to me were far worse and painful than being called a slut, Sal" She began on a drunken rant. Sal calmly sat there and listened for about half an hour while she rattled off reasons for how much she hated Fred, now her ex-boyfriend, and now herself so much for ever considering him to be worth any effort at all. She shivered as she once again vividly remembered the ugly words and encounters of that evening she had desperately tried to totally clear from her mind.

The last few weeks had been utterly perfect – or so she had foolishly thought simply because Fred had been nothing but sweet and attentive, and he continually telling her how hot she looked was definitely something she could get used to. Also, they had spent nearly every weekends since he had taken her out on a wild duck hunt around at the ranch of the father of one of his friends for the first time doing fun, exciting stuffs like mock shoot out games at amusement parks, poker, truth or dare, river diving etc. Then they would make out passionately for hours, taking full advantage of the fact his parent's motor home when they were not around. Could life get any better? Then on the particular evening Fred had invited her to the frat party at a special guest house, she had never been happier. She had made sure to dress well for him and had arrived early so she and Fred could enjoy each other's company. At a point they had separated and she went into one of the restrooms to ease herself. The females being occupied, she had quickly dashed into one of the males. Not long after, some of the party members walked in and they started discussing. It was there that she had overheard some of Fred's friends talking about her like she was a fresh meat to devour. And they added that Fred had boasted that she would soon be the first black pussy he would taste and plug, thereby adding her to his lists of sexual conquests. After she made sure the boys had left the restroom, she had gone to seek out Fred with a very heavy and sad heart. Eventually he cornered and caught him actually groping some loose looking girls and he had denied that he never had anything doing with them, and that he was just fooling around. They decided to go to one of the rooms. She strongly confronted Fred on the stuff she had heard in the restroom. Fred easily laughed it off, stating that why would she believe two drunken idiots. He then cupped her face and solemnly declared his love to her once again. Then they started kissing and making out. Now that she was thinking about it, she shivered in disgust at herself.

"Mmmmmm, that feels good," Yvonne had moaned as Fred flicked at her earlobe lightly with his tongue before moving to suck the side of her neck, causing her to writhe against him in pleasure, her eyes shut as she revelled in the sensations he provoked in her.

The feel of Fred's cool hand against her skin, sliding its way up her shirt jolted her out of her reverie as she remembered the words of those boys in the toilet. She quickly wriggled away from him, removing his hand from under her shirt with her own.

"Hey there, easy big guy!"

"Aw c'mon babe," Fred pleaded, nibbling at her earlobe as he spoke.

"No, I told you, I'm not ready yet," she said, placing his hand firmly on her hip.

"Oh, fine," he grumbled, his facial expression indicating his general displeasure at the situation.

Yvonne &leaned in and kissed him lightly on the lips.

"Awww, don't be such a sour puss. Let me make you feel better." With that, she kissed him again, this time a longer, hotter kiss, full of tongue. She had just begun to lose herself in the kiss when she felt Fred's hand move away from her hip and back to the hem of her shirt.

"Fred, cut it out! I told you, I'm not ready!"

His reaction caught her off-guard. His face had become dark with anger, and, without warning, he had caught her hands and pinned them together in one of his. Suddenly she became acutely aware of how powerless she felt, especially when she took Mike's masculine physique into comparison. Her heart began to race as she mentally tried to calm herself down, trying her best to school her fear.

"You little bitch," he growled, "you've been nothing but a cock-tease these last few weeks and I've been patient with you, but I've had enough of your fucking bullshit. Someone needs to teach you a lesson."

"You like that don't you, you bitch. You pretend to be so innocent and pure but I know you're begging for it, you're fucking begging for it. I can see it in your eyes."

"Fred leaves my hands this instant or there's going to be trouble for you." She warned.

He once again looked her up and down, but this time with a sudden look of disgust and irritation, "Well you are not really worth the trouble anyway. You are only just a black piece of pussy whose sole purpose is only to be fucked, though not even for sucking anyway."He finished and threw her hands away like it was trash. Then he had stood up and ordered her out of his room. Before that though, he made a call for more babes in his room. It was so surreal for Yvonne that her brain and body simply refused to function and move. Fred promptly took hold of her stunned self and practically threw her out himself. By then it was already past twelve in the night and towards the time when the rainstorm started picking up. She had walked like a zombie to her car and didn't focus not until the rainstorm eventually began.

Now inside Sal's kitchen, she still struggled to think coherently, to articulate the shame she was currently experiencing, but her mind had gone blank. It seemed as if she had shut down completely, become incapable of thought or action, almost as though she were observing the scene from afar, icily detached from everything around her. "Yvonne?" Sal's voice sounded puzzled and genuinely worried.

"Sal, I know you probably don't want to talk to me but please, you have to listen to me."

The desperation and scared tone of her voice brought Sal to full attention.

"Calm down Yvonne. You know you are yet to tell me what actually transpired and went wrong at the party? You have been staring into space since you started speaking" he asked in a soothing voice.

"Oh, Sal, he...Fred...I can't...can you please just forgive me?" Her voice broke as she tried to get the words out, and she began to sob hysterically.

Yvonne's heart raced. Not only did she currently have Sal right there with her, mere inches away, but more importantly, she had to apologize. Before her courage failed her completely. She took a deep breath and then began; nerves making her words come out in a rush.

"Alright, I don't have the foggiest idea on where to start, yet I simply need to state that I'm sincerely sorry.

You were right about Fred, and I should have listened to you instead of getting angry with you, and I'm sorry I've been a bitch, and I no longer deserve a friend like you, that is, if we even are still friends."

The burden off her chest, she began to cry again. Sal sat in stunned silence, unsure of what to say next. He wanted to tell her how he had worshipped her and always would, how he wanted to make her tears go away, how he forgave her because that's what friends do, but he didn't know where to begin. He got lost in his thoughts and didn't realize how much time had passed until Yvonne's tearful voice pierced his consciousness.

"Sal? Please, say something. Please. Anything."

He turned his head towards her voice.

"Yvonne," he said, gently, "of course I forgive you. You are as yet my closest friend and companion, presently and until the end of time."

Totally caught unawares, he didn't see her practically lunge for him, wrapping her arms around him ecstatically, hugging him tightly.

"Oh Sal," she whispered, "I'm so, so sorry."

He pulled her back from him, and reaching for her face, felt where the tears were falling and wiped them away softly.

"Shhhh," he whispered. "It's ok, everything is ok."

Seeing now how much he indeed cared and watched out for her, she once again flung her arms around him tightly as she dissolved into tears again. For a few moments, Sal didn't say anything, but merely held her, stroking her soft hair with one hand and whispering soft, reassuring noises into her, rocking her back and forth. Finally, Yvonne broke the silence.

"Thank you so much for always being there even when I was not," she whispered against his chest, moving slightly to wipe away the tears that were still streaming down her face.

"Are you hurt?" The concern in his voice and the fiercely protective look on his face melted her heart, causing her to dissolve into another round of tears. Here he was, her knight in shining armour, even after she'd been such a bitch to him. And he had been right all along, and she hadn't listened to him...she felt like the slime of the earth but at the same time, had become gradually aware of how good it felt just to be held in Sal's arms. How comforting they felt around her, how it felt like nothing bad could possibly ever happen to her as long as he held her.

This last thought gave her courage, and so she finally replied "No. Just badly shaken."

Relief flooded through Sal's body. He hugged her even more tightly, then pulled back, saying, "C'mon, let's get you comfortable and tucked in."

She tried to get up by herself and immediately felt a little unsteady on her feet, no surprise given the heels she was wearing and the considerable alcohol she had consumed in her grief. Yvonne didn't say anything, but allowed herself to be lead inside the room, and felt comforted by Sal's body heat next to her. Instinctively, she laid her head down on his shoulder, snuggling in closer, and though the feeling of her head on his shoulder filled him with joy, he schooled his emotions.

This is neither the time nor the place to feel like you've hit the jackpot, he chided himself. She needs you, she's hurt, and she's vulnerable. Control yourself. So he settled into his place, contenting himself for the time being with wrapping a protective arm around Yvonne. He enjoyed the sense of peace and calm being with her like this brought him. Once they had gotten inside the house, and he placed her on his bed. He stood to leave her but she couldn't bear the thought of being alone, so she slipped her cold hand into his warmer one, and felt a surge of happiness as he squeezed her hand delicately and started to rub it. This invigorated her more and her body began to feel warm and mushy all over. She gasped and gave a soft but audible groan as she failed to make any attempt of removing her hand from his.. Sal didn't quite know what to make of this, but certainly did not feel like complaining, so did what he felt she wanted at the time without questioning her. But he had to get things ready so he told her he would shortly be back, that he wanted to clean up in the kitchen. She begged him not to be long and he smiled in agreement. Sal threw the empty ice cream tub away, washed the glass and spoon and then made his way over to the bedroom. Thinking she was already asleep, he made for the love couch in his bedroom. He was immediately stopped by her voice that she knew he was dodging her.

"Or is it because I have touched Fred?" She asked with another sad, tearful face.

He was quickly by her side and held her hands, "No never. How could you even think that, Yvonne? I just wanted to give you privacy that's all."

"Well there is still room enough for two here so you can join me." She said and tapped the position beside her.

Sal gulped and eagerly joined her after switching off the TV. She instantly drew closer to him once he lied down beside her. He pulled the duvet over them and wrapped her up in his arms.

Yvonne was not so sure what woke her up- the steady throb of her headache or the dress that was squeezing the life out her. Sunlight flooded the room and she rolled over to face the other way. She tossed and turned for a moment but didn't want to disturb Sal who was still asleep on the other side of the bed She sneaked out of bed and into the washroom, practically stumbling over the heels she had been sporting the night before. As she looked at her reflection she laughed, and then cursed herself for getting so upset over a guy who just wasn't worth it. Then she found a way to get out of her dress, and stood there examining herself in the mirror. Yvonne was slim and petite, one of those women who was so effortlessly comfortable in her skin that nobody could help but be taken in by her grace and confidence. Her hands slid over her flat stomach, and down to the black thong, which she quickly stepped out of. Her hands reached back as she unclasped her bra and let it fall to the floor, unleashing her perfect round cocoa breasts. She searched the cabinets under his and her sinks and found an unopened toothbrush. She brushed her teeth, jumped into the shower and washed all her troubles away. She smiled contentedly at the goodness in being within a safe and genuine company.

After slipping into Sal's favourite old T-shirts, which hit her mid-thigh and was therefore, she reasoned, decent, she began cooking breakfast. The smell of a fry up reached the bedroom door, which she'd left slightly open and Sal woke up with a big smile on his face. Saturday mornings had always been the highlight of his week. It made him remember then when they were really close, he and Yvonne would meet for breakfast to discuss antics from the night before and plans for the evening ahead, and then go for a run or hit his gym at home.

Even before he entered the kitchen, Sal knew that Yvonne was already in the room. Inhaling deeply, he breathed in the fruity scent of her shampoo and the food she was cooking, heard the soft tread of her footsteps on the kitchen floor.

Studying her for a while before clearing his throat, he uttered "Hello there Yvonne."

He didn't see it, but the sound of his voice made her jump, but he could hear that she had been startled when she replied, "Oh! Sal! Hi!"

He chuckled softly. "I scared you, didn't I?"

"No you didn't!" she protested.

"Of course I did, I can hear it in your voice."

She made a face at him, sticking her tongue out.

"Alright, fine, I finally accept. You terrified me."

That was one of the things she had missed about their relationship, it still unnerved her that he could intuit her emotions with such unerring accuracy. She knew she ought to have gotten used to that by now, but it always got to her all the same. All her life, she had always felt that Sal was the one person she could be completely honest with - not only because she had known him as if they have been together since childhood, but because he could do what he had just done. No matter how she was feeling, he knew it just by the sound of her voice. More importantly, she knew that amongst all the guys she knew, he was the only one she could be certain was friends with her because of who she was, or even what she actually looked like. She knew she attracted plenty of male attention because of her adorable doe eyes, her long, curly and wavy black hair and her slim but curvy, figure, and though she enjoyed the attention, it still made her sceptical of any guy who tried to get too close to her. Except for her latest goof with concerning Fred. But right now and with all what had recently happened to her, she believed Sal was the only one worthy of her, body and soul. She bit her lip as she stared at his wet body.

"I thought I'd bring you breakfast in bed, to say sorry for being such a mess last night..." Yvonne said when she heard him walk in.

Sal swallowed hard noticing the way she never really 'said' anything; she purred it. Noticing how incredible her body looked covered only by the thin layer of white material. It never ceased to him how someone so slim could have such a womanly figure. He shook his head at himself. It was first thing in the morning, and his cock was in control of his brain.

"Don't mention it. Do I have time for a quick shower?" Sal asked, hoping she hadn't noticed the growing erection tucked away in his pyjamas.

"Your house, your rules" she teased as he ran up the stairs.

By the time he came down fully dressed, she'd prepared fried eggs, bacon, sausages, toast and baked beans. Sal threw the towel over the back of the bar stool next to him, as they sat at the island in the kitchen. "You know, it's not good for the wood if you leave a wet towel on it all day." She said, picking it up and throwing it at him.

"What happened to my house, my rules?"

They laughed as they ate breakfast in a comfortable silence. Sal cautiously asked how she was doing, and she smiled back at him and told him she felt surprisingly good. And she did. Fred had been the biggest and most messy mistake of her life which she passionately wished not to make again. Now she realized that despite his antics, Fred was as fake as they come.

She accidentally belched and looked back at Sal with a guilty look.

"Oops." He said

They both erupted in laughter. She was now indeed with her truest friend and now she had come to stay and never to let go again.

Yvonne quickly got used to her new lifestyle and would now frequently visit and stay with Sal in his apartment. Their friendship and bond now started to wax ,ore stronger than ever before. She still regretted what she had done to Sal and would always ask for his forgiveness but Sal had insisted that she should drop it and that she should know that they are now ore than friends and it would more than a lying, worthless shit to take that away from them. And so they had smoothly glided to the way things used to be for them before the coming of Fred into their peaceful lives. Yvonne was now convinced she was where she should be. Her affections have now transformed into something else. The very feelings and emotions she had been hiding deep in the deepest recess of her heart and now willing to explore and experience with her best friend Sal.

Sal on the other hand has been tying his utmost to be the perfect gentleman towards Yvonne ever since the incident has now promoted her to frequently visit him in his house. Even though he knew quite alright that the feelings for his best friend still run hot and true still, but he was not even sure whether she was now ready to express her real feelings to him now that Fred was finally out of their lives. He would sometimes stare fondly and dreamily at Yvonne while she was doing something either in the kitchen or closely with him on the table. She would catch him staring at her several times and he would immediately avert his eyes and pretend to continue doing whatever he was doing at the time. She would smile and also stare at him when he was not looking. Though both of them were still tentative in their mannerisms, body language and looks towards each other, but there was no denial that a chemistry quite different from their normal relationship was already brewing between them and it was just a matter of time that their feelings of subtle but obvious attractions would inevitably draw them together. Though there were unavoidable instances where each would accidentally come into very close contact with each other. There was an instance when Sal and Yvonne were both cooking in the kitchen and she suddenly slipped on the floor with a startled cry. And of course Sal, the ever ready gentleman that he was, had instantly rushed to her side, continuously asking if she was okay and all that. Yvonne had moaned and gritted her teeth in pain as she felt the sharp pain of where she had scraped a side of her knee against the kitchen counter. Sal had consoled her before going to get her a first aid. He had washed and dressed the bruise with ointment and lightly applied other antibiotics. All the while he was doing all these; Yvonne had started looking at him with a funny look as he dressed her little wound. She could not deny the tingling feeling his fingers were giving her as he talked. If Sal had noticed, he would have seen her lightly shivering as he did what he was doing. Though one would have Thought it was the pain that was actually making him do that but in reality it was the way Sal's fingers kept working on her skin, sending shivers of excitement over her body. After a while Sal had noticed she was not responding the way she should and looked up to see whether she was truly okay. Their eyes had met and they were locked on the spot as they stared at each other, each breathing deeply and watching for the next move and yet none deciding to make the first move or anything at all.

"You sure you are okay?" Sal asked and broke the ice.

"Yes I am fine. I am just feeling kind of woozy from the fall I had, nothing much really." She said.

And yet they continued looking at each other, the air hot and becoming heated and thick with a sexual tension around them. He kept staring intensely at her sinfully lovely face and lips, wondering how sweet her lips would taste like if taken. Yvonne too on the other hand had started breathing heavily, feeling a deep yearning her like never before. She looked at his fit, powerful body hidden behind his loose cotton shirt and unconsciously licked her lips. Both boy and girl continued to stare at each other in anticipation. Each wondering who would dare take the first move.

Is this right? Should we be doing this? Surprisingly Sal's inner voice was the one troubling him from deep within this time. But Then again he looked at her back at her perfection: her adorable, black doe eyes, straight, lovely teeth, pert, full chocolate breasts whose bit could be seen under her slightly unbuttoned blouse, her so lovely wavy, curly dark hair. He did not know what she was feeling either but he just could not shut down the voice and deep yearning in his swooning head. He really wanted her right there and then but he still restrained himself. He would have taken that move that would finally seal a romantic fate on their relationship but he does not want it to look like he was taking advantage of her emotional situation. Yes, he knew quite alright that it was not as serious as he was taking it but he was still not sure yet on the position of her feelings.

Yvonne stared into his lovely and vivid blue of his eyes they now blazed with obvious passion. Though she was still curious about what was actually going on through his mind right then as his eyes continued staring at her. God she had never felt so much passion and hunger from an ordinary stare before. It was as if he wanted to devour her there and then but still restraining himself, kind of like he was still waiting for her answer.

'Needing me hungrily. Waiting for me badly' She thought

She wondered in frustration on why he was not making the first move even now that they are free. How could he not know that she had started feeling the same way about him?

And once again they were interrupted by the droning sound of the boiling kettle and each had to separate for the time being.

Sal cleared his throat stood up and smiled, "Hope you can still manage to eat?" He asked in amusement.

Yvonne rolled her eyes and laughed at his joke, "Yeah right. It was only my leg that got bruised not my mouth, smart ass."

They both laughed and returned to finish their cooking.

Sal and Yvonne continued to hit it off despite their hide and seek affection for each other. They started hanging out and going places of interests as well. Though both of them were not really big party goers, especially for Yvonne ever since her traumatizing episode with Fred. They mostly prefer hanging out preferring going to the movies and avoided parties, especially frat organized ones like a plague. They would drink, mostly light beer and juice in public but normally strong stuff or a bottle of good wine in his apartment whenever they order take out or pizza. Even though they were the best of friends before but their bond had become closer and thus were now inseparable. Both of them became officially labelled as a couple to everyone with some even making comments of "finally" "at last" etc even though when they both know they had not taken the step to consummate such approach to their relationship. But it was totally a sort of rarity for them not to be seen without each other despite the difference in their faculties. Soon after the last semester exams they had planned to finally go on short trips to see their families together. It was even around the time towards Thanksgiving, and they believed there were no other perfect opportunities than that period. They sat to thoroughly plan the trip together and Sal suggested they first visit her home first. They went home together to her my family's home and they stayed Tuesday and Wednesday night. It was really a fun time for both of them, especially Sal and it was exactly as if he was around his family. To her consternation, Yvonne's little sister, Emily, was on Sal throughout the time, bugging him with all sorts of questions that were supposed to be above her age like asking since when Sal has been in love with her sister, what kind of girls he likes, how he had been coping with the ladies on campus despite his hotness, how often he takes her sister on a date and if he has a handsome brother like he is. Yvonne was practically trying to shut her up all of the time but it was only futile. Sal, on the other hand, was clearly enjoying himself and tactfully answered the inquisitive questions from Emily as best as he could. It was really a fun time for him and Yvonne could see that. Despite her earlier trepidations, she was very happy at how everything has turned out. Her parents were absolutely taken with his charming and gentle demeanour and behaviour, well maybe the exception was her devilish little sister who kept trying to embarrass her with her daring barrage of questions. But all in all It was fun for everyone and they really enjoyed themselves. It was a little bit of surprise though when Emily had insisted that he stayed with them some more. Sal had promised her to be back very soon, and without Yvonne so that they could have their own personal outing like she wanted. Yvonne had informed her parents she and Sal would also be stopping over at his home before going on a little road trip together. Once Tom, Yvonne's dad, had a little bit of man to man talk with Sal, he bid them to be careful on their little journey. While Yvonne's mom, Sheila, made sure to load them up with her irresistible, freshly baked buttermilk muffins and chocolate and peanut cookies. So on Thursday they left for Sal's home and by their calculations intended to spend the weekend there before finally leaving for their real journey of hiking. Sal's parents were very ecstatic to see their son and they welcomed and treated both of them to a feast fit only for kings. Sal's mom, Amanda, could not just get over how pretty and adorable Yvonne was. She made sure Yvonne was stuffed to bursting as she kept making sure her plate was filled over and over again. Sal's dad, George, was quite amused at the way his wife was behaving to Yvonne and he knew with a mix of sadness and joy that part of the reasons why she kept doting on Yvonne was that she saw in the girl the daughter they were never able to get. She almost always whined him to death about not having a daughter she could preen and decorate with her countless ornaments. Sal was equally very happy at seeing his mother engaging in something that was making her livelier in conversation for a while now. Though it was not as if his mother was the naturally gloomy type, well far from it. In fact she was almost always the livelier between her and his dad. His dad was as quiet as he was but necessarily firm when it comes to important matters. He was also a very intelligent business man whose success was evident in his real estate business. He had really also tried at being a good and responsible husband and father to his family. His mom was also a priceless gem to them all. During those rough start of the years when his dad was still struggling, his mom Amanda has always stuck with him through thick and thin. She in return had tried being a good wife and eventually mother to their only child and son, Sal. She had supported her family with her mini jewellery business before her husband hit his breakthrough in the recent booming real estate and property business. Though they had tried to have another baby but due to the unfortunate state of Amanda's complications that nearly ended her life during her last birth in which the twin sister of Sal's twin came out as a stillborn and Sal almost did not survive, she was medically advised not to have another baby in order to greatly reduce the risk of death. She had been so very heartbroken at first that she nearly turned to a recluse. But her husband George, God bless his soul, had made sure to keep and nurse her back to normalcy. She eventually got over it and threw everything she had in bringing up Sal in the normal, parental as best as possible. She also endeavoured to Love her the more. She knew it must not have been easy at all for him during the crises of her brief but harrowing emotional breakdown. She also fully focused on her jewellery business because naturally she was a hardworking woman who has always believed in a woman making her own money and not solely relies or mounts her burdens on her man. Together, they had been able to achieve so much that they were not lacking in anything ever, and despite bringing up their only son and child Sal up in affluence and wealth, they literally made sure to help him grow up to the easygoing, strong and focused young man he now was. Looking at him now, he was the perfect mix of personalities from both of them. The quiet but focused attitude of his dad and the strong but ultimately caring character of his mom. Now that he has finished his sophomore year and would soon be graduating in a year or two very soon and with brilliant prospects ahead, they can now confidently relax back and gently watch their adored son grow up to the man he wanted to become with the guidance of their instilled discipline. Though at one point, they had been comically worried that he was not even going out with any girl as a young adult man. Yes, they might look disciplined, reserved and classy, but that does not mean they are naive or unaware of how things should definitely be for a man or woman's life should flow in life. If there was anything the Trents are sure about in life, it would be that life itself was meant to always be lived as balanced as possible. Just because one has the intention of achieving academically or financially does not mean that such person should totally neglect the other important aspect which is the social life. Social activities, like Amanda would point out, are those necessary foundations of determining who we are, how we want hope to be something or somebody and who we shall eventually become. Sal has especially held on to that philosophy and with that has always tried to be the reasons that a person believes not all human beings are unrepentant jerks or murderous animals with higher brains.

Now that he was home with his parents, already halfway through with college, already a budding inventor and businessman, and to top it all equally coming home with a nice and pretty young woman, there was nothing more n  they think they could ask for at the the moment. After dinner, Sal had gone in expected with his dad to have a father and son talk while Yvonne was directly carted away by Amanda to go enjoy a nice, good soak in a bath before continuing on their girly talk.

While inside his private study, George had poured both himself and his son some shots of his favourite Butterscotch rum. He had him get a seat beside him as they talked.

"So how is everything going with you son? What are really your plans now after college?" He asked.

Sal took a sip of f the buttery alcohol and replied, "Well I hope to start my internship with any of the software giants after the completion of my degree and used that to gain the necessary experience and skills to polish up my knowledge in the area of my discipline d. And while doing that, I will be working more on my intended inventions and see the ones I could patent, sell out and own joint ownership to. Though I already have some talks in the works but I do not want to rush ahead just yet because I would really love to to take my time and study things well before jumping ahead. Career Decisions can be very dicey at times and one can never be always too careful. So after all considerations, I would select which one that might suit me ultimately in the end: either working full-time for any of the big guys in software engineering or taking the bold but uncertain leap of establishing my own start up. Though I would love to work first and see how it goes."

His dad nodded in approval and lightly smiled, "Hmmm I am impressed, son. It seems you have clearly laid out your plans for the future. And I can tell you that you have your work all cut out for you boy. That is good I must say. You have clearly gotten my head for envisioning a future of career and business projection and your loving mom's strong willed attitude. That is good. And if at any time you need any advice whatsoever from both of us, you are always free to ask us at any time, alright?" He said and patted him on the back.

"So". He continued. "How are things going with your girlfriend? Are you guys good with each other?" He asked.

"Well I can assure you that everything is perfect dad. And for your information dad, she is really not my girlfriend yet. Though we have actually been very close friends since our freshmen year. And we recently just net started to get very closer. We are still exploring nothing actually and see where it goes. But she is really a nice and caring girl. And also the most beautiful I have ever seen."

His dad chuckled in amusement and took a drink, "Damn son I think you are really in love with her. Well that is not a bad thing anyway. I remembered how I felt about your mom when we met, and ever since then we have always waxed stronger. I really hope you guys find what you seek with each other. The bond your mom and I share with each other is something that just cannot be explained until it is actually felt or experienced."

Then he went ahead to pat his son on the back, "Love is Avery beautiful thing p, Sal. And as long as you guys give it time it will surely come to you. If you are assured she is worth it then there is nothing wrong in giving it a try with yourselves. You guys should only try and be careful, alright."

Sal gratefully thanked his father and they moved on to other topics.

Yvonne on her own side was already done with her bath and was now sitting down and chatting with her best friend's mother. They had quickly warmed up to each other and gifted away. Yvonne clearly impressed Amanda with her informed knowledge on ornaments and jewellery. She had asked her where she got such knowledge from and Yvonne replied that she usually visited her father's late mom who was a jeweller then when she was small. She narrated how the shiny stones then used to fascinate her. To the great amusement of the grand mom then, Yvonne had called the jewels 'the fallen teeth of the gods' when she was told how valuable they were. Amanda had helplessly shaken with laughter at the funny descriptions. Yvonne was equally amused and shook her head at herself for ever coming up with that kind of funny, ridiculous name. Still shaking with mirth, Amanda had concurred that the name, even though funny, had somehow been appropriate in a way because it could be assumed the parts of a god, dead or alive, would definitely be very valuable. They had discussed more on dressing styles and the matching jewelleries with them. It was quite the enjoyable time for the two ladies as they bonded more with their conversations.

"Yvonne I would only be lying if I say I have not been enjoying your company. You are kind of the daughter I never had. But I would like to ask you a very important question and I really hope you would be sincere with me. Are you truly in love with my son Sal just like the way he obviously loves you?" She asked as she watched Yvonne closely.

Yvonne sighed and looked down, "To be honest Mrs Trent, I do not really know how to define the feelings for your son but all I know is that I do care about him. Though recently our feelings for each other have started developing into something else. We have been the best of friends since our first year and it has been challenging. Though I would not deny that Sal's feelings have been running deeper than the normal friendship level and I have started feeling the same way too. We have fought, disagreed and almost got separated as friends but here we are still waxing stronger. All I would sincerely say about us now, Mrs Trent, is that what we have been having together is not just love but something made stronger by the trials and sweetness of friendship. And yes I can say it anyway that I am now truly falling in love with your son, and this is not only because of our friendship p. But Sal is the sweetest, caring, strong willed, and lovely young man I have ever known in my life. Even though we have always been there for each other from the beginning like I have said, but the true reality is that he has always been there more than I am. And as everything stands Mrs Trent, I would love nothing more other than to be the love of the life of your son if he would now let me. All I want from him now is just to to say it to me with his own mouth. Then I would really be proud to formally become part of your honourable family." Yvonne finished, already tearing up with emotions. She was now remembering all what she had done to Sal during her brief run in with him. She was still ashamed of her action back then. She had been lucky to have t the loveliest of birds around her and yet still went ahead to hunt the ones in the wild. Though she was aware that Sal really loved and cherished her, hence the strong feelings of affection he always displayed around her. All she wanted was for him to make the first move and utter the words out of his own mouth for her not to have any doubts again on how he still thought of her, especially after the Fred episode.

Amanda, seeing her distressed, state quickly moved to sit beside her. She took her of her hands in her own and said, "Awww please find it in your heart to forgive me, Yvonne. I never meant to upset you. My question was only asked out of motherly love and concern for both my son and you. I want you to know that you are a sweet girl to be with, at least with the little I have seen today. And never blame yourself on the past because it never does good but only unnecessary regret. We all commit errors and it is better and prudent to lift ourselves up and gain from them. It is even the best if We have good people around us to see that and still help us to be better persons from whatever r mistakes we might have made e, either accidentally or not t. I love my son and always trust him to make the right decisions for his life e inn whatever way that i is right but that does not mean I do not wish the same for the lover r of my my son. I like you Yvonnee, be rest assured d of that. Love is a funny deep feeling and does not need to be rushed.. I believe you guyss are adults and old enough to make your choices but please both of you should try and not break each other's hearts. Love yourselves truthfully either as friends or as lovers. But whichever way It goes, I want you to know that you are r always welcome here any time and any day Yvonne. You are family now."

Yvonne looked up at her in gratitude and hugged her tightly, "Thank you so much for the kind words. You have no idea how much they really mean to me Mrs Trent." She said with a voice full of emotions.

Amanda laughed lightly in reply, "Nah it is nothing Yvonne. And please you can call me Amanda, okay. Remember I said that we are now family."

She helped Yvonne wipe off her tears and they laughed and went outside to join the men back.

The weekend flew away quickly for them and Amanda was actually pouting and wishing that they should still stay more. Sal and Yvonne had both promised they would be back soon. They also gave their reason of not being able to stay to the very limited amount of time they had left before resuming for the third academic session and they still had spots to visit before the occasion break passes. They bid their farewell but not until Amanda had gifted Yvonne with some beautiful 'teeth of the gods' to both women's amusement and secret joke. The women had reached had promised each other to now frequently communicate as the men watched on in amused silence. Afterwards, everyone finally parted ways.

Sal and Yvonne now started their journey to the place they had both planned to go for a vacation in the Kauai Island after the exams. It was a nice vacation place popularly named as the 'garden island' and they were really looking forward to enjoying their time together for the first time as friends. .. On their way to the airport, there was an awkward silence in the vehicle as Sal drove on towards the airport. They had decided to take his truck due to its big and roomy features and they were both glad they did as they were now laden with several gifts from the visits to their respective parents. Yvonne was really feeling uncomfortable with the silence, and being the more outspoken one between them was already feeling as if she was being eaten out of the insides. And just as the silence became too bearable, she turned to speak to Sal but only to discover too late that he had already been nursing the same thought.

"So what do you think?" They accidentally said in unison and then laughed.

The formerly tensed and awkward mood in the truck has lightened up with that simple blunder and opened a way for a normal conversation.

"Sooo what do you think, Yvonne? I mean about the whole thing with our parents?" Sal began cautiously.

Yvonne shrugged, "Well nothing much. Just happy that everything went well, eventually. So what was your dad's opinion about me? I have really been curious I must confess."

Sal chuckled, "Well there really was no special thing that was said other than that we should only be careful and that we must make the right choices together."

"Oh that is nice" Yvonne replied softly.

"So". Sal continued "I guess you did not have any trouble with my mom."

"Oh not at all. She was cool though. I really like her. In fact I really love your family Sal. Thanks for a good time."

"Well no problem. I t was also very nice back at your place too. I really hope to see and taste more of your mom's peanut cookies though. They are really very nice." Sal smiled

Yvonne giggled warmly and then screwed her face into a cute pout and frown, "Well I can as well make butter muffins and peanuts cookies, you know. I never even knew before and you never bothered to tell me."

Sal shrugged but laughed, "Hmmm I never realized you are that talented. I think starting from today I will hold you up to that. But is that jealousy I detect against your mother, Yvonne?" He asked and looked at her, his face now screwed up totally in mirth.

Yvonne punched him playfully, "Yeah it is jealousy. Well my mother is sure a good cook, likewise yours. She almost drowned me with affection all the time we were at your place." She said, smiling fondly at the memory.

They made more small talks and jokes until they reach the airport. The matter of their hearts still being ignored deliberately by both of them. But both knew it was a matter of time their hearts would be decided finally soon when the situation comes. The journey to Kauai was almost uneventful as they were already exhausted from their road trip. They slept throughout most of the journey until they reached Hawaii. They quickly took a cab to their destination hotel. Their trip was a sort of co-sponsored one by the Hawaiian tourism state as one of their yearly tourist packages for American students. Both of them had been able to sign up for it earlier and were able to qualify for the trip. All they did was spending just a bit to cover our personal expenses while the rest was paid for by the state. So that means they had to share their allotted room m with some other students who were able to qualify for the package. But eventually it was lots of fun as they went scuba diving, played beach volley ball and other games, participated in a funny shooting game known as crazy shooters were teams of students were pitched against each other in a mock battle using mud pellet guns. There was tug of war, roller coaster rides, fun poker, arcade games etc. There was also a little exploration of parts of the islands they had organized among themselves. Yvonne was so happy and excited because it was long since she had this much fun. What further made e made everything special was the fact t that she was finally enjoying great outings with her best friend. Though many at times they had shared hungry and passionate stares at each other whenever they come across a couple or students making out. They knew they needed to talk but were still stalling and no private place yet for them to due to the activities because they wanted to make sure to use the opportunity of the co-sponsored trip as much possible. The chance encounter did not happen until one day, the chance opened for them. They had gone to get ice cream and on coming back their crew had left them behind in the room. . They had quickly rushed over and traced them based on direction towards where they were last seen... They made a mistake and got a little bit lost in one of the restricted topical gardens of the island and seeing that there was nothing they could do again in tracing them, they had then decided to explore the restricted area. They came to an area with waterfall and bright foliage and flowers. There were some peacocks and wild birds. It was indeed a beautiful site. Though they knew the e were already trespassing on a private garden but they were so tempted to keep exploring. They splashed around the waterfall and sat down just to admire the whole stunning natural scenery. They had been watching peacefully in silence until Sal suddenly dropped the bomb.

"Yvonne. I love you" He had said abruptly while looking forward.

Yvonne turned around incredulously, "Sorry I don't get that. You are saying?

Sal was facing her directly now, "I said I love you Yvonne "He repeated.

Yvonne was so happy inwardly that she does not know what to do to the point of being speechless. They continued staring at each other intensely and Sal once again made the bold step towards her.

"I have loved you ever since we started as friends and up till now as friends and more. And I hope you give the lost ship of my heart to enter the harbour of your heart with love. So what say you my lady?" He finished and courtesied.

Yvonnee was about answering when they were interrupted by approaching footsteps. They quickly hid among one of the foliage and allowed the people to pass before making a run for the exit. That had been a close call for them. Unfortunately, they did not have the opportunity to talk further as they got embroiled in last minute activities before their stay finally expired on the tour. By Sunday everyone had gotten ready to depart to the respective destinations they came from. It was a really lovely time for both Sal and Yvonne as they were able to make more friends and learn about other new things from student and people alike.  They had flown back from Hawaii down to the place a where they had placed his truck for safekeeping. And from there went back to Sal's apartment. Both of them had been preoccupied with what has been placed on their minds since Sal's statement in Hawaii.. They got back home and unpacked their stuffs from the truck upstairs to the apartment. It was another thirty minutes later that they were able to finish. Once they finished, they were so tired but happy after the successful end to everything. Sal quickly went to shower first. But as he was about coming out of the bathroom, he suddenly heard a loud, frightening scream. He more than literally stumbled over his feet in the mad rush to quickly get to where Yvonne is and saw her at the balcony, staring into the obviously deserted street. It was already evening and darkness has already descended to cover streets and alleyways in its shadow. He found Yvonne still shivering and he immediately embraced her

"Hey what is wrong? What did you see?" He asked as he patted her terrified body.

She could not say anything at first but after she was able to calm down due to Sal's comforting hug and caresses, she began to talk.

"Sal it was Fred. I swear I saw him. It was him. Oh Sal you....you ne...Need to have seen the way he.... he oh god....he was just standing there staring at at me with an evil grin. I... I swear Sal I saw him right there. He was standing...he...he"

"Shhhshhh it is okay. I have got you. It is okay. Here why don't we go inside? It is getting kind of cold and creepy here." He said and led her back inside.

He quickly made her a steaming cup of honey and ginger tea to calm her nerves. He looked around and made sure everywhere was locked and secured.  After that, he gave her the drink and made her take a considerable amount of the sweet and aromatic beverage, he sat down beside her and asked what really happened.

Yvonne took a deep breath and sighed before she began, "As I was waiting for you to get done in the shower, I suddenly felt a sort of cold breeze and the creepy feeling of being watched. Then I walked to the balcony to get some fresh air and look around. Then I suddenly saw Fred standing there alone on the street watching me with a kind of evil grin. It was his eyes that terrified me the most. They were gleaming with a mad, murderous intent. He also looked haggard and scary in a terrifying way. It was when he suddenly pointed at me that I lost my composure and screamed. I have never been so terrified like that in my life Sal. And again on looking at where I saw him, he was not there again. He has simply vanished into thin air and that was the time you ran out of the shower to come to me..I swear Sal, I was not imagining things. I am very sure it was him. I just hope we are safe Sal coz I do not know what to do." She started shaking with fright again and Sal had to quickly calm her down.

He earnestly guaranteed her nothing would occur and he would ensure nothing definitely happens to her. After he was sure she had calmed down, he urged her to go shower so as to cool down. Once she got into the bathroom, he took his combat cudgel and his secretly kept Swiss combat army issued knife he had bought online some months ago, made sure his balcony door was firmly locked, he took one of his small but powerful torchlight, securely locked his apartment door quietly so as not to let Yvonne know, and quickly proceeded to make a thorough search of the building's nooks and crannies. He inspected his truck at the parking space downstairs and saw it has not been tampered with. He also searched the other parked cars but could not find anything. He asked some of his neighbours he saw loitering around downstairs if they had seen anything strange but none of them claimed to have seen anything. So if at all Fred had been there, he has surely disappeared without any trace of him again. He quickly went back upstairs to his apartment while making a last sweeping search, lest Yvonne started panicking at not seeing him around in the room. He quietly unlocked his door again, hid back his knife and cudgel at a secluded but nearby place around his bed and made sure his door was firmly locked. He was microwaving the cheeseburger they had bought while coming when

Yvonne finally stepped out of the bathroom. She now looked more lively and calmed than the way she had been several moments ago. She sniffed in the smell of the warming burgers and only then realized how hungry she was. She smiled gratefully at Sal and sat down to eat with him. After watching their meal down with freshly squeezed orange juice, they had both cleaned up and retired to bed. Sal made a last minute check of his locks and doors before going in to join her in bed. He faced the other side to the door and watched for a while. He turned around to see whether Yvonne was sleeping and he saw her staring at him.

"Hey there. Thought you were already asleep." He said softly.

She shook her head in response, "No I could not sleep yet."

He reached out to flick a lock of her hair from her left eye.

"Hope you are feeling better now?" Sal quietly asked

"Yes I am good Sal. Thanks for everything" She whispered.

Sal smiled happily, "You are always welcome, Yvonne. I....."

"Yes I love you too Sal. I always will." She suddenly uttered, shocking him for a moment.

Sal thought he was hearing something else. They continued staring at each other for several minutes.

"Yvonne I'm sorry can you repeat that once again, please?" He asked, his voice clearly ringing with doubt.

"Yes you heard me right Sal. I do love you. I know you may find it difficult to believe but I have also been in love with you longer than I can remember. It just took me so long to admit it to myself and realize it. I believed our relationship is enough for both of us and should not be spoiled. But the recent events and everything happening around us have made me realize that nothing is going to be ruined about our relationship. I already know where I belong now, and that place is with you." She finished and surprised him the more with a firm kiss on the mouth.

It was as if Sal was in cloud nine. He would have believed he needed to pinch himself if not because of the physical touching of their lips already in sync. It only took a few minutes for Sal to reboot his brain before he stretched his arm and drew her closer to him in order to explore her warm, sweet mouth deeper. Their tongues started duelling vigorously against each other. It was as if they needed to sate a deeper hunger that has always been there in their bodies. Sal unconsciously groaned in pleasure at his dream of making Yvonne his own finally coming true. He massaged her back as they continued to taste each other's mouth. She deeply groaned and crushed herself against him. They separated for a while to catch their breaths, their eyes glittering with the passion of their love and lust for each other. Sal kissed her mouth one more time and slowly kissed down her neck. She closed her eyes in absolute pleasure as he licked and kissed her lobes and inner ears. He slid down and rubbed her fresh and juicy looking bosoms through the light, cushy, material of her night robe. Thankfully for Sal, the robe was easy to open for him to access her womanly treasures within. He could already feel her hard nipples through it and he licked his lips of the saliva that was already dripping from the hungry grip of lust and anticipation. He first removed his own pajamas top to get more comfortable. Even the air from the air conditioner could do nothing to dissipate the heat that was beginning to radiate from their bodies. Yvonne shivered in excitement as she viewed his fit, muscular body. His handsome face and lovely blue eyes twisting and shinning with a strong passion and love for her. She moaned in excitement that a man so good and nice could hunger for her so. He bent down and deeply breathed in her alluring scent of Jasmine and the hint of her womanly essence. He growled like an animal as he bared her chest open to feast on her perky, cocoa breasts. Her breasts, though not that big, were perfect on her chest. Her dark areola was really wide and her nipples very thick. He gently cupped and caressed them, rubbing and gently squeezing as she moaned and thrashed on the bed. Her thick nipples have always been sensitive and could make her cum from his touch alone. He rubbed and twisted her nipples, making her buck in ecstasy. Not being able to wait any longer, he bent down and started feasting on them with a wanton abandon. He made love to her breasts in such a way that she started shaking with mini orgasms. He glided his tongue all over the tip of her left breast before taking the thick nipple into his mouth and sucked like a hungry infant. He would lightly chew on them with his teeth in such a way with his teeth before gently blowing on them with his breathe, thereby creating a cool, tingling sensation on her nipple. He was also busy massaging the flat of his Palm on the other breasts and using his fingers to actively strum her nipples. Once he finished with the left breast, he placed his mouth on the other one and eagerly gave it the same treatment. Yvonne was already a shivering and crying mess from all the passions and ministrations of Sal. Her whole body was tingling and she could feel her thighs getting more wet and sticky from her now running juices. Unable to wait to taste her any longer, Sal removed his pyjama trouser, his thick cock throbbing and dangling with thick precum spouting from its head. He opened her robe finally and watched her lovely ebony body with adoration and more lust. The air in the room was now thicker with the scent of their bodies and that in itself was making him go crazy. Her svelte, dark body was already pulsing with pleasure and he could see her trimmed pussy hair was matted to a shiny gloss with her liquid essence. Her inner thighs really wet and sticky the juices. He moaned and licked his lips as he wasted no time in dipping his head down to get drunk on her essence. He breathed in her heady musk and started licking away like a cat would lick off a delicious cream. Yvonne cried out at the new sensation as Sal licked all over her pink flower with a feverish passion and hunger r . He suddenly took her legs over his shoulder and, drew her closer and plunged his tongue into her tight, wet treasure as he ate her out to stupor. She shook violently as she screamed, this time with a thunderous orgasm that caused her ears to start ringing with tinnitus. Once he had satisfied his thirst on her juicy pot, he wasted no time in cradling her to his body in a sitting position and entered her in a deep, long stroke. Her mind and body lost to the pleasure, she literally shed tears of joy and passion on his shoulders as he continued to rock her back and forth on his cock. He drew back her head for a kiss and she groaned wantonly in passion as she shared the taste of her juices on his mouth. He went faster into her as he gradually felt his balls boiling with cum. She bit on his shoulder as she once again felt a building storm of orgasm, this one different to the last one. Sal moved his hips a little bit faster as he sensed their rising climax together. Not being able to contain themselves , they both raised their heads in the agony of pleasure while joined together as they screamed their sweet release as one. She had a little faint as her pussy literally contracted around his cock and squirted clear, thick fluids noisily over his laps, balls and sheets. Sal in turn shouted like a feral beast as he erupted his thick, seamen into her sucking pussy. Their combined juices were so much that they poured out messily on their bodies and onto the sheets. Yvonne kept on shuddering and groaning as they descended from their sexual pleasure. It was a night they would forever remember as the most passionate and enjoyable ever to finally turn their friendship into something more beautiful and precious. Sal managed to change the sheets before they wrapped their bodies around each other and slept off.

# THE COMING STORM

The following day was like a whole new beginning for them as they started the new session. They made love once again in the shower before they departed for lectures. Sal had suggested she transfer her things to his apartment so they can as well start living together. Yvonne had happily agreed to that and promised to visit her dormitory so as to finally move her things from there. For the first time in her life, she felt truly alive and happy and she vowed to make it count for her and Sal. After the lectures, She went straight to her room to start arranging her things.

She did not see Fred smile maliciously and leave after watching her as she entered the building.

Yvonne hummed happily to herself as she began to arrange her things and d know the ones she would be taking with her to Sal's place. Fifteen minutes into her arrangement, she heard a knock on her door. Thinking it was her probably her roommate, she went to unlock the door.

"You did not even call....." Her statement stopped in mid sentence as she saw a strange lady in front of the door. What even made her stranger was her unusual height and stunning beauty. She had pale skin like the colour of fresh milk and blood red hair. Her eyes were shades of deep emerald and seemed to be staring into her soul. But what Yvonne sensed to be particularly unusual and strange about her is the kind of sexual appeal she was effortlessly oozing. It was like her scent and aura was creating a sort of special pheromone-aphrodisiac that would make anyone easily want to sleep with her. She just could not explain it. Her tight red tank too barely restrained her big blobs. Her long skirt was skilfully slit on both sides to show her fresh, sexy pale thighs. She must have really turned a whole lot of heads while coming here, Yvonne thought.

The lady spoke for the first time after a few minutes of looking into her eyes, " Good afternoon Miss. Please I am looking for a Miss Yvonne Roberts. Am I by any chance speaking to her?"

Yvonne, now more suspicious, despite the strange, horny feeling she was getting from just looking at the woman nodded, "Yes indeed you are. So how may I help you?"

"Do you know a man called Fred? I think I may have something very important about him that I want to share with you. May I at least come in?"

Yvonne, now more intrigued about the lady's statement, quickly adjusted her body for her to pass. The woman smiled turned ominous as she let herself in.

*******************************************

It was very late by the time Yvonne got home to Sal and he was already worried sick after all his calls to her went to voicemail. He tried to talk to her but she was just too tired. Though he felt a bit hurt but immediately shrugged it off. He did not need any negative thoughts at this point in their relationship. The next day, Yvonne had already gone even before he woke up. He also noticed that some of her things were no longer there. He was so baffled that he could not at first comprehend what the hell was wrong with her. And so with a heavy heart, he prepared for lectures for the day.

Yvonne became more and more distant to him and he started seeing that what was happening was no longer a joking matter. He would ask her at times if she came to his apartment, and she would only say she was alright. That there were certain tasking projects her department was doing lately that has been affecting her focus. She would smile sweetly and apologize, promising to make it up to him. Sal would keep quiet, but he knew the smell of bullshit if He sees one. He had tried to make love to her several times but would suddenly turn aggressive, stating she was not in the mood. At times she would be gone for days without coming to his apartment, calling him nor be seen around the campus. Sal now knew that his best friend and girl were in a trouble of sorts and he was helpless in finding what kind trouble it was. One day after visiting her dormitory room and finding nobody there, he had tried her mobile but she was not picking. He suddenly became dejected and frustrated that he started weeping in pain beside his truck. He looked up once again to stare at the building and was instantly shocked to see Fred grinning at him from a distance not far to the dormitory. He gritted his teeth in anger and run after him. But before he could get to him, he had already fled and disappeared. Sal was irate to the point that he truly yelled out in torment. He could bet everything he has got that Fred knew about the strange behaviour and recent disappearance of Yvonne. But as it was he could not do anything about it.

He kept on visiting the dormitory until he hit the jackpot one afternoon. This time around he had let himself in to even know what was going on. Yvonne had given him a spare key to her room in case of emergencies. And now he was glad that she had done that before. He inspected the room closely and he discovered that everything was intact and tidy. That further gave him the conviction that she had been coming to the room frequently. He was however surprised to see many feminine sex toys and whatnots on her mirror stand. He was about inspecting them when he suddenly heard approaching footsteps. He quickly ducked into one of the wardrobes and fervently prayed that he would not be caught. He had barely hid himself inside the wardrobe when the key turned in the lock from the outside and two females entered. He thanked his stars that he had smartly removed his own key from the lock after he entered. But he soon got the shock of his life when he saw Yvonne entering with a strange lady. He at once noticed something attractively strange and ominous about the pales skinned woman. She had an imposing height and domineering air around her. And she was very, very, sexy and captivating in an unearthly way. Yvonne on the other hand looked like a shadow of her former self. She now looked like a zombie and hovering around like someone one drugs. He was alarmed and shock at her transformation. She was almost looking like Fred even. Yes Fred, the bastard who was still a thorn in their flesh and had caused this. He swore to find the bastard and exact his revenge on him.

The pale woman sat down and commanded Yvonne to massage her feet and legs. She then ordered her to stop, and grinned wickedly as she started stripping herself naked slowly. Yvonne, now watching her with a rapt attention like a slave watches a master, started breathing and moaning deeply as she watched the woman undress. Once she was done, the woman spread her legs wantonly and commanded Yvonne to start eating her meal. Yvonne, who was by now shaking feverishly from uncontrollable lust eagerly pounced on the woman's bald smooth, pussy. She giggled as Yvonne slaved at her wet pussy. The more she produced, the more Yvonne licked her up. It was a hot lesbian scene that elicited horniness. But it was the woman's pheromone pervading the room that was further making his cock becoming harder than a rock. It was as if a powerful aphrodisiac was being released. The woman's voice was a sultry mix of husky and eerily deep. She later pushed Yvonne away and went to pick a big strap on dildo. And Sal was treated to the most wanton scene of girl on girl sex he has firstly ever experienced face to face. It was as if Yvonne was thoroughly enjoying herself as she kept on squirting and cumming copiously as the red hair fucked her pussy mercilessly. After she was satisfied with her work. They cleaned up and lefty the room again for God knows where. But before they left, the pale woman looked at where he was hiding and gave him a wink before they left and locked the room. Sal was so shaken that he hurriedly left the room and raced back home. Even though he was feeling all sorts of emotions like: confusion, anger, betrayal, irrational lust for the strange woman and a strong overwhelming sadness. He had noticed one thing though as he witnessed Yvonne's lesbian act, and that was despite the fact that she seemed to be enjoying herself, she was still in pain. There was a haunted look in her eyes that was screaming for help. He sighed but resolved he would definitely get to the root of the matter. He stripped, and took a long, nice time to get cleaned up in the shower. Then he retired to rest for the night.

It was midnight and the night was stormy just like the night Yvonne had come into his room after her breakup that fateful night with Fred. He was also experiencing the same ominous dream like that night only that he was having sex with Yvonne in his room. It had looked like he woke up in the middle of the night only to find Yvonne, bright and pretty like she used to be before the appearance of the pale lady and she had begged him to come meet her in bed. He had gladly obliged and slide into bed with her. He had asked her why she had decided to leave him and she said she would never leave him again, and have come to stay forever. He had hungrily taken her lips and they started a slow and sensual lovemaking, with him eating out her strange smelling but delicious pussy vigorously. He was so unusual ly horny that he came heavily into her. But even as he came he noticed a change on his body. He became very fatigued and collapsed back on the bed. Looking through his unfocused eyes, he saw the pale white woman laugh at him before disappearing from his room. He did not even have the strength to think before he collapsed into a tired deep sleep.

The next day he woke up, he truly felt like shit similar to a hangover. He looked at his face in the mirror and cried out in shock as he saw the haggard look he had got overnight. He shook in fear and for the first time realized how bad the situation he and Yvonne found themselves. He quickly freshened up, dressed and went out to a more public place in town among people because he was now fearing to stay in his apartment. He started browsing on demonic spirits or evil creatures attracted to sex. But the facts he got on the two most popular sex demons: the incubus and the succubus did not point out any features of either of them sleeping with both men and woman at the same time. Frustrated and lost, he went to a bar and stayed there till evening. By the time he left, he had gotten so drunk that he could not even differentiate between his fingers again. He was walking without direction until he stumbled into a strange carnival and circus show at a big park. He walked drunkenly for a while until a tent caught his attention. It seemed to have no sightseers or fun seekers so he entered. The room was dark and gloomy until candles suddenly lit up around him.

"What brings you here, young man?" A deep, motherly voice seemed to ask from the dark fringes of the tent.

He opened his mouth to speak but could only retch heavily onto the floor. He looked up and the world swam before his eyes. The last thing he knew was someone approaching him from the darkness before he slumped and fainted. He woke up with a start and looked around. He seemed to be in a tent. He was about questioning himself how he had gotten there before he remembered. He looked around and saw an old woman with a face like leather. He thanked her for the hospitality and was about leaving when he was stopped cold by her next words.

"How did you got tainted by the Sarakesh, young man? The stench is all over you. And do not worry; I have given you something to stop the spread of its poison. That is how it likes doing with its prey. Marking them and killing them slowly through sex" She said and stared at him.

He shook with emotions as he started narrating his ordeal and how it all started. The woman had listened to every word he said till the end without uttering a word. Then told him  to bring his girlfriend without fail or else he would soon lose her to the evil spirit forever.

"And remember that there is a big price to pay if you hope to save your lover. The person who summoned it shall pay the ultimate price with his life for it is inevitable. No one can ever hope to control such hideous creature. So quick off you go before it is too late."

Sal did not know whether it was mere luck or a suddenly descended divine providence that made him to suddenly locate the strange old woman. He took note of the location of the circus and park and left immediately. He took a cab straight home and quickly arranged the things he would use to be able to get Yvonne because he strongly suspected she would not leave with him willingly. He tried her number first before deciding to go to her dormitory. She didn't pick so he immediately ran down to his truck and rode down to campus towards her dormitory. He fervently hoped and prayed that he would see her tonight. He could not believe his luck when he suddenly found her some few blocks before the administrative building. He took the prepared syringe, hid it and came out of his truck.

"Hey Yvonne. Yvonne please stops. I really need to speak with you" He said as he ran after her.

She stopped and slowly turned to him. She had been shuffling like a walking corpse when he found her. But looking at her face now, he nearly cried out in pain at what she had become. But he had a mission at hand..

"Yvonne can you hear me? I'm right here" he said again and switched the syringe into his hands

She looked in confusion but still tried to speak, "S...Sa.....Sal is...that you?"

"Yes it's me baby. Please you need to come back to me. Let me love you like before. Please don't leave me Yvonne."

There were tears running now on her cadaverous looking face. "No I can't". She replied. "The mistress forbids it. Save me please Sal. I am in pain." She sobbed and covered her eyes.

Then she looked up, her eyes starting to lose comprehension again. She smiled and managed to wave at him, "I love you Sal. I always will."

Sal, weeping himself replied, "I love you too Yvonne but I won't allow you do this. Never"

Then he swiftly grabbed her and plunged the syringe into her neck. He quickly carried her unconscious body into the truck and drove like a demon towards the park while still maintaining the speed limit. He got there, hoping the old woman wasn't a mirage as he picked up Yvonne's weightless body on his shoulder. He almost sobbed in relief when he located the tent. He was surprised to see one other woman with the old woman. He instructed him to lay Yvonne down on a prepared runic drawing and started the ritual in earnest. She warned Sal that he should be ready to witness and partake in some certain sexual rituals. Then they asked him to strip naked. After making some unknown arcane chants in undefined language, they sprinkled everyone, including Sal with a very strong essence. After performing more chants, the old woman stripped. Sal was disgusted at first but was totally shocked to see her body firm, smooth and supple. If she noticed Sal's surprise, she did not acknowledge it. She and the other woman started kissing and sucking each other's tongue. Before long they started sucking, licking and fingering each other. They then took wooden looking phalluses and began to fuck each other in the sixty nine positions. She beckoned for Sal to come and start jerking off before them. Already horny, despite the seriousness of the situation, he started jerking off to their sexual display. Soon his thighs started shaking with an oncoming climax. Sensing his impending release, the two women quickly knelt before him while still fingering their now very wet pussy. The wet, squelching sounds of their pussy and the overpowering smell of all sorts of pheromones in the tent soon drove him on edged as he released copious amounts of sperm on their faces as both women also moaned their release. Afterwards something very unnerving to Sal happened; the women glowed sharply until the bright shone to a blinding proportion before it winked down to a very small ball of light. The light hovered briefly in the air before it went right into Yvonne. She gave a sudden cry and her body started to convulse. Then before Sal's unbelievable eyes, she began to fill up and transform back to her pretty normal self.

"Do not rejoice yet" The Frank voice of the sexy old woman cut his joy short.

"You still have one more sex ritual to perform and that is sleep with the doppelganger of the Sarakesh that is now hibernating in your wife. Now you were lucky to have been able to capture it while it was in this state. So now once your wife transforms, have sex with her no matter what you see. Only by this last sexual act can you save her life." She said.

And not long after, Yvonne had transformed to the pales skin lady before transforming into something hideous and ultimately scary. It was the true form of the Sarakesh; somewhere between a spider and octopus. He hesitated a bit.

"Do it now" the old woman shouted.

Steeling his mind and bringing up a picture of Yvonne. He lied down on the creature and started pumping away. It was only its sexual pheromones that kept him going as the subconscious state of the creature wrapped its arms around him in pleasure. He continued to think about Yvonne until his cum churned out of his balls and he came like a roaring inferno. He was surprised to have produced that much cum in such circumstances. He gradually felt his spirit leaving his body through that release till he faded to unconsciousness.

Sal woke up feeling really strange and off. He stretched and twisted his body only to discover that he we simply not Sal anymore. He looked down at his chest and almost screamed in panic when he saw he had grown breasts and a pussy. But on looking closely he, he saw with dawning realization that he was actually in Yvonne's body now. He touched the breasts and immediately felt pleasure as the tingles radiated throughout his body. He looked around and saw nobody around. There was no old woman, her young accomplice or anybody for that matter. He searched around for some clothes and saw some already laid out. Curious to know more, he touched his pussy lips and clit and gasped in pleasure at the feeling. So this is how women feel, he thought. He quickly dressed up and went in search of Yvonne, not knowing how or where he would start explaining to her.

Yvonne now Sal looked on as Sal, now Yvonne was trying to put on one of her high heels. Despite being in a woman's body, Sal has not gotten used to it due to his conscious feeling as a man. After strutting like a new born calf, to the absolute amusement of his old body, she dropped the high heels in frustration.

"Aww darling now you know what we ladies go through to look beautiful for you" mocked former Sal

"Oh really. Then how about I expose this body right now to wipe that grin off your face?" former Yvonne grinned mischievously as she start a little strip tease.

The former Sal rolled his eyes, "Please be careful how you want to start using that sexy body. Remember it's still mine and I've got your balls with me" he said menacingly.

Former Yvonne continued to grin as she slowly exposed her breasts and began cupping them for former Sal to see. Then she totally stripped down, sat down on a chair and sensually caressed her pussy lips,

Former Sal dropped his hands helplessly and moaned, "Oh fuck this. You win this time honey" He eagerly ripped off his clothing.

Former Yvonne's mouth moaned as she saw the lust on her lover's face. They fell on top each other and instantly connected.

Former Sal looked at former Yvonne's face, "Together inside each other forever. You are mine and I am yours" They kissed as they began to explore their new bodies together.

■■■■■■■■■■■■■■■■■■■■■■■■■■■■■■■■■■■■■■■■■■■■■■■■■■■■■■■■■

Four days later, Fred's body was found in an alleyway and according to investigations, he looked like he was sucked dry to death with his trousers down and his dick stuck in a hard on till death.

It has been over one month since the ugly and supernatural incidents with Fred. Sal and Yvonne had picked up the pieces of their almost shattered lives and friendship and are now gradually getting back to the normal pace of their former activities. Though it was normally felt as weird at first, being in different bodies and trying to feel your way around at becoming a female or trying to be a male. Even though their souls and personalities have perfectly fitted into their newly allocated bodies, but there were still body and word mannerisms both are yet to adapt to totally. On the day after the totally weird night their body transformation took place, Sal (now in Yvonne's sexy body) had immediately searched for the whereabouts of his girlfriend (now in his old male body) and had found the body naked and still out cold under a tree. Sal had first exhaled a discernible breath of alleviation before continuing to wake her up. Even after Yvonne had woken up from her very deep sleep, still groggy and disoriented, she immediately knew that something was off as she was staring at her former feminine body. Stunned and confused, she tried rubbed the sleep from her eyes as she looked at the state of semi undress of her own body due to the casual and flimsy state of the shirt showing an almost clear outline of breasts and nipples. And as if the already felt confusion was not enough, she had started having an alien male sexual feeling which just does not make any sense to her at all. Her eyes widened in sudden realization and she jumped up with alarm to inspect her body. She gasped as she gazed down at her masculine body and a cock getting hard and dangling between equally looking masculine legs. Deciding she had really seen enough, Yvonne gave a scream of horror but soon cut herself shut when she heard the deep tone coming out instead of the shrill, feminine one.

"Somebody should please explain what the hell is happening to me? And how have I suddenly got a dick while getting aroused by my own almost naked body now standing before me? She asked as she raised her voice in apprehension.

Sal had to calm her down by briefly telling her the harrowing details of what happened and how they had gotten where they are. He told her they had to get home and relax so as to properly soak everything in. And afterwards, accepting the reality of their switched identities became a gradual process until it became a normal thing. And now they are bringing their relationship to a new, exciting level, more so for Sal whose personality is now very eager to explore the sexy body of his partner who has always been the girl of haunting his dreams. The new Yvonne has now finally moved to the new Sal's apartment as both of them have agreed to live together as roommates and share the costs. It was now the beginning of the third academic session which makes it their final year in college. The new Sal has been receiving tutorials from new Yvonne on how to go about living his life, especially concerning his intellectual works and the research he has been doing. Likewise the new Yvonne has been learning how to imitate the real Yvonne's mannerisms and preferences. They knew they would have to go to their homes sooner or later and they dread making blunders in front of their families or raising suspicions from them. Both of them knew that there are now aspects of their lives they can never hope to get back and all that was left for them to do in order to protect their secrets is to pretend nothing happened and also try as much as possible to blend in. But all this did not stop them from passionately exploring each other's new body with lustful vigor. By now even their colleagues and distant friends are now fully aware that they are inseparable and loved up.

In the beginning though, they had at first given each other some space so as to adjust and give themselves the necessary time for making the reality of their current situation to properly sink in. It was still surreal for them; like having an actual alien being living with them. There was also that feeling of awkwardness in both of them, like having that nagging feeling of trying to have sex with their own bodies even though deep down both of them knew they just could not stay away from each other long enough despite only trying to strictly teach themselves on how to properly live in their new lives. They tried to bury themselves in their school work but it was just the beginning of the first semester and the academic pace was still slow being the first week, thereby making them more tempted to jump on each other and wildly go at themselves with a reckless abandon. Sal's real personality kept having strong, tempting sexual fantasies of the lovely body of his girlfriend he was now occupying. Even though the physical feminine feelings and biology are all intact, but his consciousness was now getting to understand how a normal female body feels sexually and it finds that new kind of feeling strangely exciting and wanted to really explore it more with its old male body. Meanwhile for Yvonne, it was a whole lot to take in for her consciousness. She had to adjust to the overwhelming physical feelings of male pheromones, biology and urges. She would shiver uncontrollably at times when she felt her new body's urges and then would be tempted to rub and massage the body's dick. The feelings and sexual hunger would make her groan deeply in the body's male voice. She was starting to have the full understanding of the male body and now knew why most males seemed to love sex so much. She would turn in Sal's body and her female consciousness would make the body bit its lips in an aroused feminine way as it gazed on her old, sexy womanly body. But despite the physical male urges of the new body, Yvonne's consciousness could still suppress those urges with its female control. This case of hidden but mounting urges went on and on between the two lovers until the dam of passion burst on them one day.

On a particular Friday afternoon after their lectures, they had gone for a grocery run, this time in Yvonne's car as they usually take turns taking each other's cars out. The sexual tension that had accumulated over the days between them was so thick that it could easily be held and cut down with a knife. They walked the mall's aisles and shelves together as they picked what they wanted. But later on even that simple task was beginning to get cumbersome as they occasionally stared at each other with an increasingly unrestrainable hunger. What even made the situation worse were the constant physical contacts of a touch here and there as they examined and selected the provisions together. Both of them knew that each felt the tingling feelings each touch generated between them. It was as if they rushed through the rest of the shopping as both realized they could no longer hold those urges any longer. Though nothing sexual has been spoken between them, and yet it was as if they had given themselves a nod of understanding and surrender to the undeniable yearning that is now boiling for each other. They reached home and quickly managed to take in their shopping upstairs to his apartment. Once they finished, both now stood and stared at each other. Then gradually they began to inch closer to each other before running to close the distance and lustily jumping forward to ravenously start licking on each other's lips. They both moaned wantonly as the heat of lust and want to devour each other's body overwhelmed them. Then Yvonne suddenly gave a wince of pain and drew back as she tried to flex her arms and shoulders.

"Damn it. I've not gotten used to this body yet. I am still thinking I am presently in my old male body forgetting that there is only so much I can do with this one. I think I might have overstressed the muscles a bit too much while we were shopping." She said as she continued rubbing and twisting her shoulders.

"Yes your right. I can actually concur to that. Even though I always try to be cautious with the way I use mine out of instinct and habit but the male strength keeps overriding my restraints. I think the best way for now is to just go with the flow. But we shall make that problem our headache later. Now permit me to help you out with your stiff muscles, dear" Sal said, took Yvonne's hands and pulled her towards one of the living room couch.

"Aww thanks honey. That would really make sense," Yvonne sighed with pleasure, apparently looking forwards to the massage. "It's really been long since I've had a good shoulder rub. I hope those new male hands of yours would be as good as you intend."

Out of old habit, Sal rolled his eyes and gave a retort "Oh yeah? We shall soon see about that smartass."

Yvonne smiled and relaxed as Sal repositioned their bodies so that her back was to him. He then ordered her to pull off her sweater, which she did with immediate effect. She tossed it aside and was left wearing just a tank top. Sal rubbed his hands together and then placed them on her shoulders.

What followed could only be described as the most blissful and arousing seven minutes of Yvonne's life. She had had massages before sure, but there was something about the way Sal expertly rubbed and kneaded and massaged her skin that brought it to a whole new level. Maybe it was the complexity between her black skin and his white own. Or it could possibly be caused by the way his solid, calloused hands firmly caressed her skin. Whatever the case, soon not only was the pain gone, but it was replaced by a hypersensitivity that made every touch more exciting than the last. She could feel her underwear getting wet as her breathing continued to come out in stained pants as she was uttering her little moans. Sal grinned smugly as he felt his new hands easily knead and mould her soft and beautifully dark chocolate skin. He happily noticed the way Yvonne readily succumbed to the magic of his hands. He couldn't lie but it felt as if he had done this before. Yvonne was smiling as her new personality imagined what must be going on now in her old body's mind. Sal had actually massaged for some people before. In fact specifically for two girls. And that would be his ex in high school and a girl who used to be a next door neighbour he had had a very brief fling with before he met Yvonne. And it always went the same. Once his hands were on a girl, she couldn't help herself want more. But there was something different this time. It was like a shared mind kind of massage. Yvonne wasn't just any girl, and Sal didn't just want to screw her and move on. At the same time though, whatever happened, happened. He couldn't stop that.

After a few minutes, Sal decided to test Yvonne's boundaries and leaned in close to her.

"How are you feeling?" he whispered softly in her ear. Yvonne shivered from the touch of his hot breath on her now sensitive skin.

She turned her head slightly so they were looking eye to eye, their lips only inches apart, and in that moment Yvonne knew what she wanted. Ever since the spiritual swapping of their consciousness happened, she had been in conflict with herself, unsure of what she wanted to happen when they saw each other. Now though, that battle was settled, and without another moment of hesitation, Yvonne leaned in and kissed Sal deeply on the lips.

Sal reciprocated the kiss with just as much intensity, his hands moving from her shoulders to her hips. He pressed his mouth harder against hers while pulling her closer. Yvonne turned her body and pushed forward so she was laying on top of Sal as they continued their kiss, her tongue sneaking its way into his mouth. Sal smiled as his tongue wrestled with her equally eager own, and the two drew back to lay down for a few minutes, kissing and investigating every inch of skin on one another. After some time had passed, Yvonne finally pulled up and straddled Sal, feeling hot and out of breath as she stared down at him. Sal reached up and ran his hands down her sides before tugging at the hem of her top, indicating what he wanted next. Yvonne smirked as she slowly removed her top, then dropped it on Sal's face, covering his eyes.

"No staring," she said in a quiet, husky tone and undid her bra beforecasting it far aside. Her ripe, milky chocolate C-cup breasts spilled out, but she quickly covered them with one of her arms. "Ok, now you can look."

Sal could not help but roll his eyes again, this time in amusement, at the way his girlfriend was trying to play hide and seek with the old body his inner presence used to own. 'But this body still enjoys the game anyway' the consciousness thought pleasingly. He removed the shirt from his face and looked up, then let out a growl seeing Yvonne covering her breasts.

"Say please," Yvonne said playfully. She could feel Sal's cock getting hard beneath her, and as much as she wanted him to just take her, she also knew that Sal wasn't the most dominating person. So she decided to tease and push him until he was putty in her hands. Though her inner presence was shocked to really be enjoying teasing and pushing its old body in this sensual way.

Before she could realize what was happening, Sal sat up, lifted her up and over his shoulder, and carried her out of the room. Yvonne was too shocked to ask where they were going, and by the time she had recovered from Sal's sudden show of dominance, she could feel herself getting thrown. She landed with a thump on something soft, and only at that moment realized that Sal had brought her into the bedroom.

"H-" Yvonne could not even finish her intended utterance as her pretty mouth went agape as she saw Sal practically ripped off his cloth. There it was the white, rippling body that had hypnotized her when he first showed up. Sal slowly drew closer to the bed and jumped in with Yvonne. He at that point took her jaw in his grasp and tilted her head up to look at her with an intense stare.

"Yes I love being gentle but that does not mean I have to beg before getting what I want." he simply said. "I know what I want, and I take it."

Sal then leaned in and kissed her neck softly while taking one of her tits in his hand and massaging it gently. And just like that, Yvonne was turned putty in his hand. There was something about the way he touched and kissed her that was so tantalizing. He was soft, yet possessive. Now she realized as she began to experience such feelings of erotic pleasure that could only come from two truly bonded lovers like themselves that Yvonne's body was not just hers, it was also his. To use and do whatever he pleased like she can also use his own in whatever way she deemed fit. Even though they normal male and female lovers giving each other access to their respective bodies, but they are now far much intertwined than that. They are now really bonded by souls and feelings.

As he continued his relentless assault on her neck, alternating between kisses and soft bites, Yvonne decided to take a spin at giving him a feel, placing her hands on his dark body and feeling his muscles. Her moans became a bit more audible as she really began to take in his body. The way his muscles bulged with each touch, how large they looked when contrasted against her tiny hands. Yvonne had been with her share of guys before, but none of them had gotten her going the way Sal had with just his lips, hands, and body.

After a couple of moments, Sal wetly kissed down to her breasts, continuously shifting back and forth between the two as he kissed sucked and licked on their nipples. Soon he was sucking her nipples, alternating between the two and making sure that while he sucked on one, he squeezed and pinched the other. Yvonne strongly heaved and shivered at the good loving her breasts were getting. She always knew her tits were an attractive pair, but the physical Sal was all over them and practically making love to them. He was worshipping them, taking control of them.

While as yet sucking and flicking his tongue all over her areolas and nipples, Sal gradually moved his right hand down her body, moving his nails daintily over her smooth skin. Yvonne arched her back at the sudden move, her body super sensitive to Sal's touch. Sal brought his lips away from her boobs and brought them back to her neck, sucking on it while slipping a hand into Yvonne's skirt. He pushed aside her underwear and gently fingered her drenching pussy, somewhat sending a strong wave of shudders all over her body as she cried out in ecstasy.

"Hmmmm~horrrr oh my god " were all the moans now loudly coming out of Yvonne as the pleasure was gradually increasing for her. Sal covered her mouth in kisses to quiet her down a bit, and then told her to enjoy whatever he was doing and feel relaxed. After this, he went back to sucking on her neck while slipping his middle finger into her pussy. He pushed it in and out slowly, each push eliciting a gasp or moan from Yvonne as she relaxed and followed what Sal said. Her body relaxed and was overcome with pleasure, and soon she was begging Sal for more.

Sal smirked against her neck as he thought 'It is my body after all'. Then he slipped another finger into her and began to pick up the pace at which he fingered her. At the same time, he also rubbed her clit with his thumb. He also brought his mouth back to tits and took one of her nipples into his mouth, sucking on it hungrily as if trying to get something to come out.

This triple attack on her body was becoming too much for Yvonne, and soon she was moaning louder than she had thought she was capable of.

"Fuck Sal... I'm so close... don'ts- HOLY SHIT!" Alec had curled his fingers inside her, tapping her g-spot as he fingered her relentlessly, and this was the last straw for Yvonne.

"FUUUUUUCK SHIIIIIIIIIIT HMMMMM YEAAAAAH" Yvonne's back curved and her whole body shook like a winded leaf as the climax overwhelmed her like a cargo train. As she came all over Sal's hand, he slipped his hand out her pussy, but continued to rub her clit and lick her nipple, dragging out Yvonne's orgasm for as long as possible.

After about fifteen seconds, Yvonne finally came down from her orgasm and she just lay there panting and in a state of bliss. Sal removed his hand from her pussy and held his fingers up to her face. Immediately getting what he was going for, Yvonne took his fingers in her mouth and licked her juices off. Not bad, she thought to herself. Then Sal withdrew his fingers and licked off the remaining.

"Hmmm I never knew I could taste so good," Sal said and chuckled.

After he had licked his fingers clean, Sal leaned in and kissed her tenderly. The kiss was very affectionate and soft, almost familiar. After sharing the taste of Yvonne's pussy on their tongue and lips, he pulled back and stood up. Yvonne looked down and saw a massive erection pressing against Sal's sweatpants, straining to be released. Wordlessly, Yvonne slipped off the bed and knelt on the floor in front of Sal. She hooked her fingers in his sweatpants and pulled them down. What came next still surprised her despite the fact that both her inner thoughts and physical body already knew what was expected.

Sal's big cock was always a delicious marvel to her body whenever she sees it. It was at least eight inches and almost as thick as a juicy cucumber. It was red, white and veiny, with a rosy head that was oozing pre-cum. Yvonne had seen these kinds of cocks in videos, but she didn't think she would ever see one like it in real life. Looking at its hard shape resembled gazing at an eager constrictor prepared to strike. Her body was both fascinated and frightened at the same time, and she wasn't sure which half of those feelings would win out even though her inner mind felt at ease.

Without thinking, completely hypnotized, Yvonne placed her hand on the massive shaft. Her entire hand barely even wrapped around it because it was that thick. She started to gradually stroke it, her pussy as yet trickling from cumming and by one way or another being significantly hotter and wetter unlike before. The contrast between her small, black hand and Sal's massive, white cock filled her with the same arousal as she experienced when she felt his muscles, though there was a slight distinction this time as a result of their exchanged consciousness. But that situation have somehow even made their sexual passion to be more inviting, like it was begging for her to do whatever she wanted with it, and yet still profoundly intrigued in spite of definitely realizing how to handle it. Before long, Yvonne had two hands on the hot dick and was stroking it faster than previously, thereby making more pre-cum to start dripping from its angry, red tip.

It dripped onto her smooth black skin, and the feel and glossy shine of the fluid on it alone sent a fresh shudder through her body. It was sticky and so warm, and Yvonne found herself deeply craving it. One of her hands curiously moved to the tip and gathered up some pre-cum with her finger, and at that point licked it off. Her eyes enlarged as it touched her tongue, the taste being substantially more charming than what her physical body anticipated. Needing more, she fully bent down and licked the tip of the dick. Then she did it again, and again, and soon she was sucking on the tip while her hands continued to work the shaft, her tongue swirling around on it.

As Yvonne stroked and made his thick cock shiny with the suction of her eager mouth, Sal moaned and groaned his thighs and legs starting to shake from the sheer pleasure of her loving mouth. Even though her mind knew what it was doing to make its old body quake in pleasure but Yvonne still smiled happily, encouraged by his moans and wanting to experience more. Yvonne licked and kissed along his shaft, taking in his musky scent and taste, feeling every bulging vein popping against her tongue. She then opened her mouth wide, taking the massive member into her mouth. It was so thick that it barely fit, and it was so long that she could barely get more than a few inches into her mouth before she began to gag.

Yvonne still managed to bob her head back and forth on Sal's cock, taking in as much as she could, when suddenly she felt something grab her hair tightly. Looking up, she saw it had in fact been Sal, and before she could respond he began to thrust hard into her mouth, pushing his cock in further than Yvonne thought was conceivable. Before long she was choking like insane, salivation trickling out her mouth and down her jaw line, arriving on her tits. The unexpected attack on her mouth sent another rush of excitement through her body, and soon her hand was in her skirts where she was feverishly touching her clit. Sal shivered and groaned out loud like a raging bull as her tight mouth barely accommodated his cock. He glanced down and discovered Yvonne finger fucking herself. He chuckled as he pulled her face off of his crotch and held her inches away from his dick. His chuckle turned to a lusty moan as he stared at all her chests and beautiful breasts shiny and covered in her spit. His dick gave a strong nod as it spouted more thick precum to the naughty and erotic sight.

"Hunnnh....What are y-nggh!" Yvonne's effort to speak ended incoherently as she was already feeling another onrush of a strong orgasm. It was not often that she came more than once in such a short time. Actually, she had never done that. But something about the way Sal was treating her body, something actually mixed between being tender and possessive, was too much for her. Sal briefly raised and rubbed his cock, using her spit as lubrication.

"Here, why don't you have a taste of my balls?" Sal let go of Yvonne's hair, knowing he didn't need to force her to lick him. And as expected, Sal had barely let go before she shot forward with an almost alarming speed and hooked onto his balls, sucking and rolling her tongue on the full white testicles. This was always one of Sal's favourite fantasies of Yvonne doing this to him before things got romantic between them. Blowjobs were one thing, but a girl he was hopelessly in love with licking and sucking his nuts was a whole different level despite knowing that the intensity of their lusts could as well be credited to their all knowing inner personalities. But even at that, he has not been able to see any girl up till that moment who has ever orally worshipped both his dick and balls the way Yvonne was doing to him. She seemed almost obsessed with his genitals, and this only made him even more turned on and made him want to fuck her even more.

"Nggggh! Fuck yes that's it baby. Oh my god! Yeah!! Feel those balls. They're full of a fresh batch of cum that's all for you." Naomi wasn't sure why, but this was the tipping point for her. The promising thought of having Sal's hot cream jizzing all over or into her was the last straw. That was somehow just what she needed to hear, and with that she pulled her head back and let out a scream as she came for the second time.

"HUUUUUGGH OH GOOOOD!" The climax was so serious to the point that she did not even realize when she had needed to get off the floor and lay on the bed, flailing uncontrollably as her body trembled. She felt something wet splash out all over her hands, pants and skirts but she was too busy to notice.

Some few moments later, Yvonne's body gradually quieted down as her climax diminished. She groaned as she sat up and looked down, seeing that not only was her hand soaking wet, but so were her legs, thighs, skirts, panties and the bed. She had always been hearing the rumours of female ejaculation or squirting but she always concluded that either the stories were lies or the ones she had seen on porn were only staged for the camera. But clearly what she just experienced was neither fake nor staged. This was different. It was dirty. It was crazy. And she cherished it. What's more? She needed more.

Sal started to say something, but before he could, Yvonne quickly pushed off her sodden skirt and panties and tossed them on the floor. It could be heard as they landed on the floor with a wet plop. Now totally and enticingly nude, Yvonne lewdly spread her legs, showing off her throbbing wet and dripping pussy. She rubbed it teasingly as she stared at Sal, biting her lip.

"Please Sal. Do it. I want you to spear me with that beautiful, white dick of yours and turn me into your slut. Own me now with your cock lover and turn me to your slut." Yvonne passionately pleaded in need of another sweet release as she started to pleasure herself with her rapidly strumming fingers. Sal, already drooling and breathing hard at Yvonne's words and antics, eagerly climbed into bed with Yvonne and grabbed her hand to stop her fingers.

He pulled her hand away from her pussy and pinned it above her head as he leaned down and kissed her hungrily. With their tongues hungrily clashing against each other, Sal's cock began to graze Yvonne's pussy, making her squirm and moan in wet lust. She withdrew once again from the kiss and took a gander at Sal, quietly begging for him to quit prodding her. Grinning widely, Sal held his throbbing dick in his hand, placed it up against her dripping kitty and promptly moved his hips to drive into her.

The next moments were like a whirling run of maddening pleasure for Yvonne. Sal's cock threatened to stretch her apart as its thick length glided into her very tight pussy. But this wasn't a bad pain. It felt amazing. Yvonne took a sharp breath as Sal pushed further into her, and soon her laboured breathing turned into moaning once he was halfway into her. She had never felt so full before, and as she looked down her eyes widened when she saw that Sal wasn't even completely inside her.

Sal gave her a couple of moderate pushes with his dick and then paused momentarily before pushing once again into her soft but tight pussy in one powerful thrust that shook the bed and shifted Yvonne back a few bit on the mattress. Yvonne's back arched and her toes curled at the sudden action, and she was suddenly hit with an orgasm that hit her so hard, she couldn't make a noise. She just held onto Sal, silently screaming for a few seconds before letting out a loud moan.

"Ahhhhh! Uuuuuungh! Oh....ohuuhm... my.... Fuck... fuck me!" Yvonne entwined her long, sexy legs around Sal's waist, further driving him into her. Grabbing the bed with tight grips, Sal quickly obeyed and began drill her, giving Yvonne's tight, sloppy hole deep, slow thrusts that let heartfelt every inch of his dick. As he filled her over and over, he leaned down and took one of her nipples in his mouth, licking and sucking and biting it. Yvonne by now has surrendered to Sal, thrashing and groaning loudly in absolute ecstasy as she felt another stormy build up of orgasm in her weeping pussy.

Sal settled into the steady pattern of thrusting into her. He firmly but gently held Yvonne's throat as he now continued to hammer into her pussy faster. Yvonne repeatedly felt the cap of Sal's cock pushing against her cervix, causing her voice to come out in louder sobs and moans of ecstatic pleasure. She placed one hand on Sal's arm and the other on his bicep.

"Ooooohyeeeeeah...uuhm... yes ... fuck me lover. . Use me like your whore," she continued to groan and beg wantonly, eager to see Sal completely bring out his sexual beast on her. Though Sal has never really felt comfortable with dirty words during sex but with Yvonne it was strangely exciting and got him even harder. He at that point fixed his grasp on Yvonne's throat and thrusted his shiny pecker harder than before into her sucking pussy. The power was incredible to such an extent that the bed repeatedly slammed against the wall. The sudden lack of oxygen left Yvonne feeling light-headed, and this combined with the intensity of Sal's fucking was all too much for her.

"AHHHHH.....YES......MMM....GONNA....CUMAGAAAAAAI N!!!!!!" Yvonne helplessly let out a long stream of incoherent words as she experienced another amazing climax, her pussy grasping tight on Sal's dick as she showered all over him with her clear, sticky cum. As her climax ripped through her, Sal pulled out of her and dove his face down onto her pussy, licking her now very thick, swollen lips and swallowing her juices. Sal at that point took Yvonne's clit in his mouth and played with it, sucking and licking on it as it expanded and shuddered in his mouth. This abrupt attack on her love button escalated Yvonne's climax, and similarly as it died down another one hit her.

"SHIT......SHIT....         HAA....YES!         YES! LOVEEER..FUUUUUCK MEEE!!" Yvonne's whole body shook in uncontrollable passion as she sprayed him one again, especially this time all over his face with more of her thick cum.

She laid there shaking and gasping for air for several minutes, having never experienced so many intense orgasms in such a short period of time. Satisfied almost frazzled out, she raised herself up on the elbows and saw her lover licking her juices off his fingers with relish while pleasuring himself with his other hand in drawing, slow strokes.

"H-hey," Yvonne said weakly as she sat up. "That big cock... that's mine... I want more... please honey." She bit her lip as she reached out for his cock. Sal smirked as he laid on the bed next to her.

"Well if you really want it then come and get it." Without wasting any time, Yvonne mustered all her strength and gently climbed on Sal. She put her hands on his broad chest and fixed up her pussy with his wet, throbbing dick before gradually settling down her hips to smoothly slide down onto his cock. The hot, slimy sensation made Yvonne let out a loud, lusty groan as Sal filled her up.

"Holy shit," Sal moaned out loudly. "That's it baby, use your hips." Yvonne nodded and rocked her hips back and forth, groaning as she felt every inch of Sal's massive member. As she twisted and ground on him, her clit continuously scoured against his cock, and the simultaneous feelings of pleasure inspired a new string of cries from her as her juices trickled down Sal's dick. After several minutes of enjoying Yvonne's bouncing and rocking on his cock, Sal placed both of his hands on her ass, massaging it as he thrust up to meet her bounces. Soon Sal was thrusting hard into her, causing Yvonne to scream and moan as he abused her small, lithe body. Turned on more than ever by her screams, Sal smacked Yvonne's ass hard.

"Fuck! Who's a little white cock whore?!" Alec yelled as he spanked her again.

"Oh my god! I am daddy! I'm your little black whore loving white cock meat!" Yvonne replied, clearly relishing his verbal dirty talk and insult. They were turning her on the more "Please don't ever stop fucking me!" Sal spanked her one more time before taking her ass in his hands, squeezing her cheeks as he hammered his cock up into her. Yvonne tightened her grip on Sal's chest, digging her nails into her skin as she came one more time.

"Yes yesyesyes YEEEEEEESSSSSSSS!!!!" Yvonne screamed as she threw her head back and climaxed, her pussy squeezing tight on Sal's cock. All the dirty word play, thrusts, her squelching, leaking pussy, the way their body was slippery together with her cum and her face and voice continuously languishing in strong orgasms finally pushed Sal over the edge of control as he roared like a raging tornado, spilling his very warm seed like a volcano into her now very slushy pussy. Yvonne groaned as she felt rope after rope of Sal's warm cum fill her and she suddenly felt much fuller than before. Totally exhausted, she helplessly fell forward onto Sal's broad chest, resting her head there and breathing heavily.

Sal also laid there tiredly with Yvonne on top of him, twitching and moaning in pleasure as his very slimy cock throbbed out the remaining cum out of him into her her copiously saturated pussy. He looked down at her and snickered a bit. She looked completely dishevelled, her once wavy, black hair totally a mess, her body covered in sweat, lots of her cum and marked in areas due to heavy sucking. Her little, black bouncy ass had turned raw from his slaps and nails. She looked like a total whore, his whore and he loved it.

"Best lovemaking ever," Sal managed between pants. Yvonne raised herself up for a little bit, now smiling down at Sal. Then she leaned in and kissed him gently on the lips. This was probably the warmest and affectionate kiss the pair shared since she had arrived in his apartment. It was filled with love, not lust. Need, not want. This feeling was very mutual between them. They didn't just want each other. They needed each other.

After a few minutes, Yvonne drew back and beamed happily.

"I love you Sal," she spoke softly. She was taken aback at the claim she just made herself. But she immediately comforted herself because she knew what she said was actually true. And she was also confident that Sal felt the same way too because even before he said it, she knew his answer.

"I love you too, Yvonne," Sal said with a smile before wrapping his arms around her and nuzzling her with his cheek. They laid there together for a few minutes when suddenly Yvonne felt a stirring inside her and let out a small gasp. She did not realize that Sal's dick was still inside her and absolutely forgotten. She looked at him and smirked.

"Ready for another round?" she asked with a kiss on the chest.

"Always without getting tired," Sal replied, and moments later, Yvonne adjusted herself on all fours, allowing Sal to start plunging his still wet dick into her from her backside as he got hold of her hair firmly.

"OH MY GOD SAAAAAAL PLEEEEEEASE!!!!!" Both sweaty and cum covered lovers went on like this for a considerable length of time, cumming repeatedly all over each another, substituting positions until in the end both were excessively worned out to continue going. And as Yvonne drifted to sleep, warm in Sal's arms and full of his cum, all she could think to herself was that Sal was right. This was the best sex ever.

Sal and Yvonne were now officially an inseparable pair as they went about their academics. Soon it would be Christmas and they would also soon be rounding off towards graduation. Both their families now know that they have moved from more than being friends and are now much in love with each other. So it was a matter of time they probably propose to each other and everything.

Now both Sal and Yvonne have really been trying to adapt well to their new lives without making any blunder or mistake through their new inner presence. They knew they feel very comfortable whenever they are alone together but this time they would soon be leaving home for the Christmas breaks and that means staying among their families despite their current circumstance for the first time ever. They had agreed to closely be in contact with each other so as to properly monitor and guide whatever each other would be doing at home with their respective families. This means that they would need to go home and spend time with their families and they knew they had to be very careful. And so the Christmas break came sooner than expected.

They left for home and hoped and prayed their plans and months of training would not fail them.

Sal got home and was expectedly welcomed warmly by his family. He acted his role perfectly when he was greeted and excused himself to go take a shower. When he came down for dinner later in the evening, he was kind of apprehensive but he steeled himself to behave normally. He sat down to eat but his mind was getting preoccupied with whether Yvonne was actually able to play it safe without blowing away her true identity at her own home. He wondered if she was currently in danger.

"Are you okay Sal? It seems you have been kind of occupied ever since you came. Is something wrong, honey?" His mom Amanda suddenly asked.

He started due to her sudden voice. He found his supposed mom, now including his dad staring at him intensely. 'You need to have to relax or you would be the one to spoil everything you and Sal have been planning to make everything right. Never let them be onto you' Yvonne's inner voice chastised him. Sal smiled and replied he was okay. Seeing that his parents seemed not convinced and he quickly had to think of a reply to utter.

"I'm just a little bit stressed what with the coming final exams, career prospects and Yvonne. But nothing much really mom and dad. I assure you that I am definitely fine."

"Oh and speaking about your girlfriend, Yvonne, it's really been long last time we saw. I hope she's okay. And I do hope you two have finally made the right decisions on the next step to take concerning careers, jobs and relationships, especially where you are going on that with Yvonne? I hope you guys are now serious and really into each other because she sure looks responsible and such a sweet girl" Amanda had said as she continued to stare at her son seriously.

And for the first time since he stepped into the house, Sal smiled warmly and the Yvonne in his inner consciousness beamed at his mother's sweet words of encouragement. Right there, he knew his mind need not worry any longer because all is definitely going to be well at the end. Afterwards Sal shrugged off his fear and began to converse with his family the way it was supposed to be.

Yvonne, on the other hand, was able to make progress with her family. The only trouble she encountered was her sister Emily. She had been constantly giving her a barrage of questions on the whereabouts of his girlfriend and whether she would come soon. She had also seen her doing thing awkwardly at first. He evaded her questions due to the and he had  to seal her running mount with a gift of a play station vita handheld console courtesy of Sal. She had grinned when she jumped up for joy because her sister knew she loved video games. The inner Sal hoped nothing should go wrong.

She was also later called by her dad a short while after dinner, her mom having travelled to go see her ailing mother in Tennessee. Yvonne had been more relaxed concerning her own conversations with her dad. Even though the inner Sal in her body had been a bit nervous but it quickly shook it off and swore to try as much as possible to make everything work and look like normal as much as possible so as not to spoil all what they have been working on both for him and Yvonne.

Her dad poured himself another cup of tea as he continued staring at her with an unnerving kind of focus.

"So Yvonne, now that you are almost through with college, what exactly are your plans and goals concerning the future?" He asked and then relaxed back in his sit as he took a sip of his steaming tea.

Yvonne was silent for a while as she thought hard about the right words to say. She knew on that spot that any stupid statement or improperly tabled utterance from her could jeopardize everything she and Sal have been building. So she took her time and quickly made the necessary decisions to say to convince her dad.

She cleared her throat. Her father immediately raised his eyebrow at her sudden mannerism.

"Well that is strange. I have never seen you clear your throat before speaking before, or is that a new habit?" He asked in amusement.

Yvonne silently gasp as she remembered she had almost blew it by acting out on the impulse of the male consciousness in her. She bit her lip and looked up at her father again.

She smiled and answered, "Well dad I plan to start an internship that would further help shape my discipline at Silicon Valley. Sal and I have both tendered our respective applications for internship to five top ICT companies there. And we have currently received an offer of invitation and interview from three so far. So we hopefully think to have successful meetings with them soon and get selected by any one of them."

Her dad nodded and sipped from his cup again before continuing, "So what about Sal? How serious or deep are you two into each other now. Don't get me wrong though, I'm not drilling you because even God knows that you guys are adults and can really take care of yourselves, but you know your mother and I are only looking out for you, you know"

Yvonne smiled, "I already know that dad. And I assure you that there is nothing for you and mom to worry about. Sal and I love each other and we really plan to take our relationship to the next level very soon, hopefully. Sal even almost adores me more than I do him. He has also been of great help in my academics ever since we have met. So no worries there dad."

Tom smiled and relaxed, "Alright then. Your mother and I do wish both of you all the best in the months to come. I love you daughter."

Yvonne got up to hug him, "And I love you too dad. Thank you for all the support like always."

Sal and Yvonne were able to make contacts, especially through video calls at night to give each other useful tips on how to now fully blend in and associate with their newly acquired families. But apart from a little blunder here and there, they were both able to effectively make their families nine the wiser about their real identities. Such was their connected love and empathy they felt towards each other.

......... Several good months later after graduation

The mirror was as big as she was, so she could completely see herself in it. On a very big day like tying the nuptial knot, ladies really look completely happy and delightful. Her dress was pure white with a bell hoop skirt coming out of her waist and slowly going down in a bell-shaped shape to the ground. The top slowly slipped down in a slight curve to show off her beautiful cleavage slightly. Roses adorned the sleeves small white bands that rested softly on her wrists. Her skirt was pure white with plenty of tulle underneath her. Her train was long and streaming behind with a rose that connected it to her dress.

Roses gradually streamed down the train and coordinated the ones on her sleeves.

What's more, the red rose bunch that she held coordinated her dress flawlessly.

Her hair was up in a high braid with delicate twists streaming down and around her face.

Her headpiece was likewise decorated with roses and sat as a crown around her head.

She had long streaming gotten tulle serving to cover her face.

She had not yet used the uppermost layer over her adorned face yet.

She would enable her father to do that yet he hadn't come in yet.

Her cosmetics had been done superbly by a cosmetics craftsman that she had contracted only for this event, similarly as she had finished with the hairdresser who did her hair.

She couldn't accept how perfect she looked or that it was her big day.

"Yvonne," said a man's voice trembling, "you look so delightful, my child."


Tears were beginning to spill down his face as he grinned sweetly towards her.

His eyes shone with satisfaction and trouble simultaneously.

"Daddy, don't cry" said Yvonne, "you're going to make me cry and ruin my cosmetics." Yvonne was attempting her best to keep down the tears.

Seeing her father constantly made her cry.

"I'm sorry honey,"Her father answered with a shaky voice.

"I can't trust I'm going to part with my infant today.

You're not going to just be mine after today.

My daughter will be gone constantly after today."

"Daddy," delicately murmured Yvonne, as she approached her father to whip the tears away, "I'll generally be your daughter.

Yvonne's arm was through her dad's as though he was going to walk her down the passageway.

Tom continued taking looks at her through the side of his eye.

"I can't accept my child is altogether grown up and I'm parting with her today," thought Tom.

"At that point its opportunity to start the ball rolling!

This lady was Melissa, the lady Sal and Yvonne had employed to assist them with putting on their big day.

Their extraordinary day was in her grasp, the wedding organizers hands.

Sal and Yvonne had no stresses however. Why?

Since this was the lady who presented the two rights around five years prior at her father's aunty's home at New Year's Eve party.

Melissa had recently realized that Sal and Yvonne would be ideal for each other.

Both had comparable characters and were keen on very similar things.

She grinned as she took a gander at the wonderful lady, a companion that she adored like a sister.

Sal was increasingly similar to a younger sibling to her.

She just needed the best for them and realized she had done right by blending these to up.

A match made in paradise is the thing that she called it.

Yvonne and Tom strolled towards the entryway that leads them to the entryway into the foyer.

They strolled up the passage to the entryway that would enable them to go into the congregation.

She could tell he was still trying to keep down tears.

Her mother Sheila and Sal's mom, Amanda, who were both just getting back from putting finishing touches to other preparations after making sure the food, drinks and other forms of entertainment have been taken care of, gleefully waved at her as they sat down on the same line with George, Sal's father, who was also waving and wearing a very happy expression on his face. Yvonne beamed and waved back at them.


And there was also solicited Stephanie, Yvonne's house keeper of respect, likewise her younger sibling.

"You sure you are okay, love?" She asked with a bit of worry.

"Absolutely," Yvonne answered with a very happy grin on her beautifully made face.

The music began and Yvonne's four bridesmaids strolled down the walkway joined by their regarded groomsmen.

Stephanie was the lovely blonde and wife that had accompanied Luke, Sal's closest companion and cousin from the mother's side from route back.

They had once grown up together years back and were neighbours at one time of their lives.

Sal was Luke's best man just a single year prior, when Luke wedded the blonde Stephanie.

Stephanie had become great companions with Yvonne several days and was one of the bridesmaids.

She was shocking, even with her gut appearing, which was holding their kid.

It was a modest midsection of a lady who was just four months along.

She was being accompanied down the walkway by Yvonne's sister, Emily.

She was in flawless hands, as indicated by Luke.

At that point came the young lady acting as the flower girl, Sal's six year old niece, Michelle. The ring carrier was Yvonne's four year old nephew, David. "Aww just see how sweet they look together," Yvonne thought happily as she looked at them walk down the path. David was taking a gander at everybody and saying hello there. Michelle was in profound focus attempting to ensure she had enough blooms to spread over the whole length of the passageway.

The music before long transformed from a delightful processional music to hear comes the lady of the hour.

"The time has come father," Said Yvonne as she whispered gently to her dad.

With a grin and a gander at one another, they started to stroll as one down the path. Yvonne looked straight ahead. She needed to see the delightful man remaining toward the finish of the path who might before long become her significant other. Her grin became much greater. Sal was ravishing in his dark tuxedo. He was tall and attractive, much the same as the first occasion when she had met him, just five years back.

Sal was as attractive as ever. His dark tuxedo did him equity. His dark vest that she had helped him choose was straight underneath his coat. He had a dim tissue in his pocket. He stood tall and grinning. He glanced back at his best man.

"She's so wonderful," murmured Sal to Luke.

"Presently you realize what I was discussing on my big day," answered Luke.

Sal cleaned tears from his eyes as he turned his consideration back to his dazzling lady of the hour that was strolling towards him. It was all that he could do to not begin crying. He grinned significantly more the closer she and Tom got the opportunity to end of the passageway.

Before long, Tom and Yvonne had arrived at the finish of the passageway. Yvonne was remaining alongside her life partner, prospective her better half. Her grin shone brilliantly. Tears were gradually originating from her eyes as she loaded up with joy. The tears of delight were difficult to hold back.

"Great night everybody," began the minister. The minister was Sal's minister that he had grown up tuning in to each Sunday for a mind-blowing duration. Yvonne gave her bunch to Stephanie and turned towards Sal.

The minister started to talk.

"Women and refined men, I invite you to the wedding service of Ms. Yvonne Elizabeth Roberts to Mr. Sal Aaron Trent. I am going to begin the procedure to join these two in heavenly marriage. On the off chance that anybody doesn't figure these two ought to be joined, talk now or perpetually hold their peace."

"Who parts with this lady?" asked the minister.

"Her mom and I do," answered Tom. Tom turned towards Yvonne and kissed her. He set her shroud back over her face, similarly as she had asked him to. She needed to remain hidden all through the function and have her better half lift her cloak when he went to give her their first kiss as a wedded couple.

"This is the day that matches all days in your lives, Yvonne and Sal. It is the most awesome day and the climax of one relationship to start another. Both of you began as companions, and afterward became sweetheart and beau. At that point you turned into a connected with couple and that cut off the dating association. Today parts of the bargains. You cut off one association just to start another one. This new relationship is one of a hitched couple. You go forward from this day as a wedded couple, to help and love each other. To mind, strong and honest to each other. You will have your ups alongside your downs. You will have your great occasions alongside your terrible occasions. This has been an example among every one of the connections both of you have gone into together. Today begins the start of another of these connections. Be that as it may, this relationship is distinctive then the ones you were in previously. This relationship will keep going forever in light of the fact that the adoration you hold for each other keeps going forever. You step into a submitted relationship appearing to the world that you are so dedicated to each other. Marriage is an awesome thing, however it is a relationship that you continually need to chip away at all through the remainder of your lives. Also, it is currently my pleasure to start the pledges and the trading of the rings that will bring you into your new relationship as a couple."

As the minister expressed these words, Sal and Yvonne looked profoundly into every other's eyes. This was the day they had been hanging tight for. It felt like an unfathomable length of time would precede their day would come, however it had at long last come. They would before long be a couple. Nothing would ever be contrasted with this day. They grinned to one another realizing that in only a couple of moments, they will be husband and spouse.

"Presently first, we will initially inquire as to whether these two are eagerly going into marriage. At that point

I will do the demonstration of trading promises then the exchanging of the rings. These pledges are exceptionally extraordinary to this couple. They chose to make up their very own dependent on customary marital promises. These promises will initially be said by me and every one of you will rehash after me. Presently, first, I will have you, Yvonne, answer this inquiry. Do you, Yvonne Elizabeth Roberts, take Sal Aaron Trent as your legitimately married spouse?"

"I do," reacted Yvonne cheerfully.


Turning towards Sal, the minister asked "Do you, Sal Aaron Trent, take Yvonne Elizabeth Roberts as your legally married spouse?"


"I definitely do," reacted Sal joyfully.

The crowd chuckled at his reaction.

"Presently onto the trading of the promises since we are all in and understanding that this wedding service ought to go forward. So genuine are they that both of you have chosen to compose your own. They are lovely and depend on conventional marital promises taken by every single wedded couple all through the world. Presently, I will initially request that you Yvonne rehash these words after me while investigating your darling eyes." The minister instructed.

Sal and Yvonne grinned colossal grins that demonstrated the affection that they had for each other.

"I, Yvonne Elizabeth Roberts, take you, Sal Aaron Trent," said the minister.

"I, Yvonne Elizabeth Roberts, take you, Sal Aaron Trent," said Yvonne.

"Through affliction and wellbeing, through more extravagant and more unfortunate."

"Through affliction and wellbeing, through more extravagant and more unfortunate."

"Till death do us part since we have survived so a lot of as of now."

"Till death do us part since we have survived so a lot of as of now."

"I love you with everything that is in me and vow these pledges to you."

"I love you with everything that is in me and vow these pledges to you."

All through saying her promises, Yvonne delicately cried as she rehashed those words to Sal with her caring eyes looking profoundly into his.

It was presently his own turn to express his promises to Yvonne.

"I, Sal Aaron Trent, take you, Yvonne Elizabeth Roberts," said the minister.

"I, Sal Aaron Trent, take you, Yvonne Elizabeth Roberts," said Sal.

"Through ailment and wellbeing, through more extravagant and more unfortunate."

"Through ailment and wellbeing, through more extravagant and more unfortunate."

"Till death do us part since we have survived so a lot of as of now."

"Till death do us part since we have survived so a lot of as of now."

"I love you with everything that is in me and vow these pledges to you."

"I love you with everything that is in me and promise these pledges to you."

Sal battled to keep down the tears as he said his promises to Yvonne.

She was at long last going to be his significant other after so long.

"Since the pledges have been traded," talked the minister, "The time has come to trade the rings. These rings are the images of your adoration for each other. They are likewise the image of the dedication and the promise of monogamy that you are swearing to each other. At the point when you put these rings on each other's fingers, you put them there to show the world that you are in a submitted relationship forever. Also, presently, it is my pleasure to go forward with the ring trade some portion of the wedding function."

Stephanie and Luke immediately walked forward and delivered the rings that they were holding. Each laid the rings that they were clutching the minister's book of scriptures.

The minister favoured the rings and afterward went to Sal, "Sal take this ring and as you gradually rehash the words I state, slip it onto Yvonne 's left ring finger."

Sal took the ring that was for Yvonne off the holy book. He took her left hand and slipped the ring onto the tip of Yvonne's left ring finger. He at that point gazed toward the minister sitting tight for the words that he would rehash as he slipped the ring completely onto Yvonne's finger.

"I, Sal Aaron Trent, give you, Yvonne Elizabeth Roberts, this ring," said the minister.

"I, Sal Aaron Trent, give you, Yvonne Elizabeth Roberts, this ring," rehashed Sal, as he slipped Yvonne's wedding band onto her finger investigating her eyes profoundly.

"Presently, Yvonne, do likewise as Sal simply did."

She took Sal's wedding band of the book of scriptures and afterward took his left hand.

She slipped the ring onto the tip of Sal's left ring finger.

"I, Yvonne Elizabeth Roberts, give you, Sal Aaron Trent, this ring," said the minister.

"I, Yvonne Elizabeth Roberts, give you, Sal Aaron Trent, this ring" said Yvonne as she slipped Sal's wedding band onto his finger looking profoundly at him.

With that done, Yvonne and Sal looked profoundly into every other eyes with adoration. The two of them realized that they were at long last man and woman, a couple, joined forever.They were so in adored and cherished offering this minute to everybody.

They lost each other in one another's eyes, yet were taken back to reality when the minister started talking again by and by, "The lady of the hour and husband to be have decided to light a solidarity flame as an image of them meeting up and joining two separate lives into one. At my right, is that solidarity flame that speaks to the solidarity that is their marriage. Will both the lady of the hour and man of the hour's folks step up and light the individual candles that are on either side of the solidarity flame."

With this, both Sal's and Yvonne 's folks went up to the light and lit the individual candles that remained beside the solidarity flame that was in the center. After the candles were lit, the two arrangements of guardians ventured back to remain before their seats.

The minister turned to the couple "Presently, Yvonne, Sal, go together and every one take one flame and expose it together the solidarity light together. The joining of two singular lives into one represents the connection of two coming together to radiate love, unity and harmony. Two separate lives, two separate characters are joining to become one substance, one being. Continuously recall this minute and recollect that the solidarity flame symbolizes your decision to join your adoration in marriage and to join your lives in marriage. You may now go and together light the solidarity flame," said the minister.

Yvonne and Sal moved from where they were remaining at the front of the walkway towards the candles. Together, they united their individual candles and joined them as they lit the solidarity flame together. At the point when the solidarity flame was lit, they put their candles down and grinned at each other. They took a hold of every others hands and strolled back to the front of the walkway.


"Presently, with this done," continued the minister with an immense grin all over, "the way toward joining these two youngsters is finished. Through this service, two separate lives and two separate individuals have joined to turn into a couple, a wedded couple. They combined their adoration in the image of marriage. It is presently my pleasure, with the power put resources into me by the State of New York, to articulate you a couple. Sal, you may now kiss your lady of the hour!" He finished.

Sal lifted Yvonne's cover and, with his arms around her midriff, kissed her profoundly, enthusiastically, and affectionately. Yvonne kissed similarly as profoundly back, sending her adoration for him through her kiss. Their crowd emitted in adulation and whistles as the couple kissed just because as a wedded couple. He then turned them to pivot and face the group of spectators. Yvonne took her bunch from Stephanie and remained with her arm through Sal's, grinning brilliantly.


"It is currently my pleasure to present to you," sang the minister so anyone can hear, "For the absolute first time, Mr. and Mrs Trent

Sal and Yvonne strolled down the path towards the entryway that Yvonne had quite recently strolled through before as a bachelorette. At the point when they got past the entryways, they moved to one side and grinned at one another.

The day they had sat tight for had at long last come. They would now be able to start their lives all together as a couple. Now their new lives about starting with their secrets only known to them in their hearts forever.

Sal and Yvonne did not take long to start planning their honeymoon right after the wedding. They used two full days to search for a suitable honeymoon getaway; a perfect fantasy looking place for them to properly have the time to enjoy themselves. Sal personally wanted Yvonne to experience something close to magical like he once saw in his dream with her. They had been scouring the internet for the third day when they came across a very beautiful vacation village in Greece known as Santorini. Yvonne was as ecstatic as a kid promised an ice cream treat when she gazed on the picture of the Greek tourist village. It was truly a stunning sight to see even when they are yet to be there. Sal too was very impressed with the look of the beautiful village and instantly made booking arrangements for their flight and hotel lodging. They left with lots of hugs and wishes from their family as they boarded their flight to Greece. The flight was not eventful except for a short phase of strong turbulence after an hour of flight from New York to Athens but it soon stopped not long after.

Santorini was undoubtedly one of the most beautiful places in the world to go on any form of vacation. The sight was just breathtakingly beautiful and magical just the exact way the newlyweds have envisioned it. The kaleidoscopic bluffs surrounding out of the deep blue were quite artistic and fabulous just like something specifically carved by the hands of a god. The colourful ocean suffocated the caldera look of the island village in different bright expressions. Also the whole scene is further bested by floats of Cycladic whitewashed structures and buildings that abound in and around the idyllic village. With its notoriety for astonishing displays, sentimental dusks and volcanic-sand sea shores, it's not really astounding the island was noted as having such huge numbers of explorers and tourists in pail records. For them,the Santorini caldera village was truly the most emotional and romantic ocean they have ever seen at that point, thereby making their wish of a fantasy holiday to really come true. It was indeed an immense sight; a stunning, priceless painting coming alive with its dark red rocks and crystal White Sea shores.

They quickly lodged in a nice, homely hotel Sal had previously booked before gleefully going for more exploration of the village. In the coming days Sal and Yvonne really had the time of their lives and lots of sex and more sex. On the fourth day of their one week honeymoon, Yvonne had gone to one of the cafeteria to get a bowl of Greek yoghurt when she happened upon a group of ladies laughing and discussing spiritedly among themselves. At the point when she sat in the cafeteria watching them, she understood there were talking animatedly on the subject of sex. Though she was amazed at the stuffs filtering from their discussions to her ears but Yvonne still got interested in them anyway. The ladies looked to be so free and unabashed about what they were saying, something Yvonne never was. Even though she was definitely not a saint, yet she could be bashful at times especially when sexual matters were being openly discussed like this. But as she continued watching and listening to their discussions, she couldn't help but notice a stunning, red head among them. And for a strange reason, Yvonne just couldn't escape thinking about her in her head was the picture of the lady stripping and twisting with her mind blowing body. Yvonne gulped as she really began to envision viewing the lady strip off the garments to the music playing in the cafe as though she was doing a strip schedule, like removing the little tank top covering her obviously firm but enormous pair of breasts.

'Shit why I'm I even thinking this way. It's not even as if I'm a lesbian'. But she kept staring at the lady till she was sure her eyes have started boring holes in her. Yvonne gasped as the lady herself suddenly turned her head to look at her. Yvonne gulped but still continued to look on her. They stared at themselves for a while before the beautiful lady winked at her and turned back to her friends. Yvonne finished her bowl of yoghurt and ordered more for takeaway. She paid and left her table. She was almost to the path leading to her hotel when she saw the same woman coming from the opposite side. Though she was really surprised but Yvonne still waited as she could see the lady was obviously coming her way.

The lady smiled and offered her hand, "Hello there. My name is Larissa. You seem to be new around here. Tourist if I'm right?" She asked in a cute Greek accent.

Yvonne also smiled and shook her hand in return, "Hi and it's also a pleasure meeting you. My name is Yvonne and I'm here on a honeymoon vacation with my husband. Just couldn't help but listen to you ladies' conversation at the cafe. And I must say you guys were something else. I mean not giving a care in the world and having fun" Yvonne said.

Larissa gave a soft, tinkling laugh that Yvonne couldn't help but notice, "Yeah that's how we roll here. We Greek girls live life to the fullest. So we don't care about whatever anybody says."

They talked freely with each other for a while and then Yvonne agreed to take her to where she and Sal were lodged the next day. She informed Sal about her new local friend and he told her if she was okay with it then he was. Yvonne and Larissa came back after a few hours the next day. Larissa came with a special local wine made from specially matured grapes from the hills of Athens and they had fun with it. Larissa really entertained them with lots of stories and information on Santorini. Before long Yvonne, obviously tipsy, started complimenting Larissa's looks as she laughed boisterously. Sal was also tipsy jumped up to put on some music and urged all of them to dance. The ladies started dancing until Sal had to retire and admired his love and her new friend. Soon, what was at first a chaste dance between the two gradually turned to an erotic one and they started touching and caressing each other. Whether it was due to the wine or just the

General air of good feeling surrounding everyone in the room, but nobody could tell as the two women hungrily kissed at one another. Sal who had settled down to watch the hot lesbian sight was helplessly getting aroused at the sheer slutty disposition of his wife.

The ladies kisses soon turned to heavy smooching and caressing until Larissa turned it up a notch by stripping her spaghetti top gown. Yvonne's jaw drops as she lustily viewed the sexy lady bared her attractive white body, which is everything Yvonne envisioned it would be and the sky is the limit from there. She basically doesn't have a blemish to her and on the off chance that anything, it is more than impeccable. Her tits were truly enormous and firm and her areolas looked so suckable simply welcoming to have a mouth on it. Her legs are athletic and shapely and her butt is as firm as it is bulbous. Her stomach isn't just level yet nearly has all the earmarks of being strong in definition. Maybe the most amazing element is her smooth, white skin now alluringly glistening with sweat of exertion and arousal.

Larissa took Yvonne's trembling hands and gave her the go ahead to stroke her bosom. Typically if a man were to make such a grating methodology on her it would have offended Yvonne, however Larissa's brazen methodology was actually what Yvonne required, and sought after.

"They feel so decent" Yvonne said in a mesmerized state.

"Goodness, they taste stunningly better, wouldn't you like to put your mouth on them." Larissa said and urged her head in.

With that Yvonne started to suckle on Larissa's big melon tits. In spite of the fact that her tits were as delicate as two cushions, her dark red areolas were hard and extremely receptive to Yvonne's mouth. "Mmmmmm, Yvonne, you do have a decent touch hmmm." Larissa shifted her body to give Yvonne the chance to properly maul her bosoms and feed on them. Yvonne kept feverishly, exchanging the huge tits in her mouth each twenty or thirty seconds, heavily sucking and pressing on them.

"It's....it's actually been long when last I've been with a lady" Yvonne mumbled into her breasts.

"Hmmm obviously you are doing great dear, just continue to lick them like you're doing. My young ladies love to be licked." And with that Yvonne did as she was directed and continued licking Larissa's rubbery hard areolas and gigantic white bosoms. As she was adoring her bosoms, Yvonne's hands started to investigate Larissa's tight white body with her hands. For a reason she just could not get, the feel of her delicate creamy skin over her hands was sending Yvonne into a carnal, enthusiastic fervour and she stroked her skin and worked more on her caresses on Larissa as much as she could. As Yvonne grasped Larissa's enormous ass, Larissa brought Yvonne mouth to hers and they traded an enthusiastic kiss.

Larissa's full, thick lips were as delicate and ground-breaking as Yvonne had envisioned they would be and she wondered about how incredible of a kisser Larissa is. Before long their profound kisses transform into French kissing that was much increasingly energetic and jolting to Yvonne. Since that harrowing sexual trap of the Sarakesh, she had never envisioned kissing a lady could be this wanton or lewd, yet actually it was without question feeling like both. As they proceeded, Larissa pulls Yvonne's outfit down until it slid past her hips and tumbles to her feet. Larissa slowly started moving her hands upwards between Yvonne's thighs and legs till she was running her long, delicate fingers over Yvonne's pussy. Yvonne lets out a groan when Larissa's well manicured pink fingers started to investigate her pussy lips and clit. Quickly Yvonne also connected with Larissa's small, pink pouty pussy lips. Though she had a bit of pubic red hair down there that felt thick but curlier than her own, however it was still delicate to the touch. Larissa additionally appears to have a huge clit despite her small pussy lips and it really felt swollen to the touch. As their tongues proceeded to whirl and tangle before their mouths, the two raunchily scoured at one another's pussy. Yvonne could feel how wet Larissa's pussy was becoming and she was certain she would be a gusher, if not more than her own.

Sal was already naked and playing with his thick cock as he was treated to the rare feast of lesbian play by his wife. What even made the scene more erotic and sexy was the fact that the skins of the ladies in front of him kept reminding him of delicious white cream and dark chocolate. His precum was now flowing down his dick copiously and he knew that soon he could erupt if they continued to keep up with their heavy lesbian play. He could not even imagine a better honeymoon than the one he was experiencing at that moment. He shuddered as he gradually felt the oncoming rush of hot cum from his balls.

"Hmmmm....your sweet black pussy feels so great Yvonne!" Larissa moaned as Yvonne eagerly worked on her sopping pussy with her fingers. Soon Yvonne could feel Larissa also pumping her fingers faster in and out of her. She first used the center finger to make a profound slide inside between her lips and afterward Larissa added one and two all the more somewhere inside her.

"Goodness my God!" Yvonne trembled and screamed as Larissa's fingers expertly roiled her yummy insides. Yvonne broadens her legs as she stood so Larissa can slide in more of her fingers more profoundly into her weeping kitty. Obviously, Yvonne has felt a pussy previously, her own, yet she has always wondered about the diverse feel of another woman's pussy in a situation like this where she wasn't under any sexual trance from an evil creature. Larissa and Yvonne continued to battle with their fingers as they moved forwards and backwards in between their now very wet thighs, and enthusiastically shared lots of French kisses as they fucked each other's pussies out.

Sal was now groaning audibly as the two stunning beauties exchanged it with each other hot and wet. The room was now filled up with the scent of their juices and the squelching sounds of their saturated kitties.

Yvonne felt Larissa's fingers haul out her fingers, licked them and grabbed hold of her towards the bed. Spreading themselves out as they faced each other, Yvonne could see that Larissa's pussy was practically flowing with thick, creamy pussy juices. Her clit was swollen and stood out in an enticing manner to be contacted or licked and likewise her labia were similarly swollen and welcoming. Yvonne could even see her pink insides that looked more profound and shiny with her wetness.

"Oh I see you really like my pussy. Well what can I say? You can dig in." Larissa said and spread her legs wider. Her exotic accent and sexiness were mesmerizing, as though they had an unlimited authority over Yvonne.

"Yes, it's so wonderful and impeccable" Yvonne said. She crawled towards Larissa and gazed upward at her.

Larissa giggled "Well I would also like to sample your flavour too, darling."

With that, Larissa made them change positions to a very provocative sixty-nine position  and wasted no time in diving into the warm, dripping treasures of each other. Yvonne can promptly feel the warmth and wetness from Larissa's pussy as she rapidly ran a long lick from the base up to her clit and down one side of her pussy lips. At that point she moved back up the opposite side. Her pussy was salty and tangy on Yvonne's tongue in a yummy way. Larissa also tongue-fucked Yvonne. She really enjoyed her sharp taste of sweetness; a taste she has come to know several times since the beginning of her bisexual life. Before long Yvonne was diving further into Larissa, clearly nearing climaxas anyone couldher vigorous licking with each passing second.

Larissa tilted her head back in happiness and said in a low, husky voice,

"YESSSS THAT'S it lover uuugh, drill me baby with your lovely tongue, get it ingirl....Shiiitt I'm gonnacumm so good soon." She moaned and controlled herself before attacking Yvonne's juicy flesh with faster licks of her own Yvonne  returns to up to pulverize on those lovely gigantic tits of Larissa's that Yvonne  acknowledges and wants for correspondingly.

Before long Yvonne screamed straight into Larissa's hole, clamping her legs over her head as she heavily sprayed all over the lady's face. Larissa, was also not far behind, bumped her hips onto Yvonne's face as she squirted her thick juices over her moaning face and chin. They took a while to calm down before lovingly licking each other's juices off.

A deep agonized groan attracted their attention and they both turned to look at Sal now before them as he furiously rubbed himself. They smiled at each other before getting up to take turns blowing and sucking him. The black and white faces of the beautiful ladies blowing him at the same time finally drove him over the edge. He helplessly arched his back in deep pleasure as his thick sperm squirted and poured over their faces and tits. It was truly a very sexy sight to see for any man. They relaxed a bit more before Sal had a hot round of threesome with them on Yvonne's request. By the time they were finished, their bodies and sheets were all drenched in their cum. The room reeked strongly of sex and excitement but they couldn't care less as they all slumped and slept off entangled in each other's arms.

■■■■■■■■■■■■■■■■■■■■■■■■■■■■■■■■■■■■■■■■■■■■■■■■■■■■■■■■■■■■

Yvonne yawned and stretched happily as she woke up groggily from sleep. She smiled and felt whole with herself. She dropped her arms and rubbed at her chest absentmindedly when she was suddenly astonished to touch a pair of soft flesh there. Looking down she saw she had suddenly grown breasts and she almost screamed in alarm but quickly covered her mouth. 'No, no, no, this ..this could not be happening ' she thought in happy surprise. Sal too was just waking up when she quickly tapped him and pointed at her body for him to look. At first, he gave a look of indifference but which was wiped off in another few seconds as he rubbed his eyes and looked at her again clearly.

"Jeez what the hell is happening Yvonne?" He whispered as he gaped at her.

Yvonne could only shrug in confusion as she happily flexed and examined her body. But suddenly a flash of blinding light went off in their visions at the same time and it was as if they went to sleep for several moments. Then later on they woke up and it was as if only a few

218

seconds have passed. They looked at each other again, this time with confusion and sadness as they saw themselves back in each other's wrong bodies. Just as they were still thinking about what must have happened, Larissa moaned and turned from her sleep as she smiled from probably a sweet dream. Yvonne looked back at her husband and they both smiled as an idea of a probable solution started forming in their heads.


THE END

www.ingramcontent.com/pod-product-compliance
Lightning Source LLC
Chambersburg PA
CBHW031121130726

47988CB00006B/2171